CAYMAN KISS

Jaqueline Kiss

"'Twas not my lips you kissed but my soul."

Judy Garland

CAYMAN KISS

JK
BOOKS

Published by JamesCafe.com
ISBN: 978-0-9788767-6-0

CAYMAN KISS

ACKNOWLEDGEMENTS

A big thank-you to Jamie for his total confidence in my ability to write a novel. He is my good friend, my mentor, and my inspiration. An equally big thank-you to Alicia, my "Keys sister". Her creative ideas, unique female perspective, and unwavering faith in this project kept me going when I was struggling. These two special people have my deepest gratitude and respect for encouraging me to take this leap into unknown waters.

CAYMAN KISS

CHAPTER 1

The sun felt good on Julie's body. It was frigid cold at home and this vacation was exactly what the doctor ordered. Julie smiled at her little joke. She was the doctor and she had ordered up a warm, sunny beach vacation to cure her ills. So far, it was wonderful. Blue skies, white sand, sunshine, and the most glorious turquoise water she had ever seen. Julie sensed a cooling of the air and wondered why the sun was suddenly dimmed. She cracked one eye open to see if it had gotten cloudy while she was luxuriating in her lounge chair. What she saw made her sit up.

An extremely well built, light haired man was standing at the foot of the lounger, peering down at her. The sun behind him was so bright that Julie couldn't see his face but she felt his piercing stare as he looked up and down her body. Although she had a very good figure, she felt almost embarrassed in her tiny red bikini as his eyes took in every curve. Julie sat up straighter and shielded her eyes with one hand to get a better look. The light haired giant took her hand and pulled her to her feet. He slowly brushed his lips against hers. Julie felt her entire body shiver. It was a simple kiss but it was the most sensual feeling she had ever experienced.

"Come," he commanded in a soft but firm voice.

Julie had a dozen questions forming in her head, but was unable to get a single word out of her mouth. She nodded her head once and, holding his hand like it was a lifeline, walked back toward the hotel. The lush foliage surrounding the four star hotel went unnoticed as they walked up the sandy path, then down the tiled walkway past the pool. The chatter and laughter of the pool patrons was nothing but background noise now. The only thing Julie could focus on was the extreme heat radiating from his hand into her hand and rapidly diffusing through her entire body. Her skin was flushed, her nipples were hard, and she could feel a heaviness building in her lower stomach.

They reached the elevator at the end of the walkway and it opened for them immediately. They stepped in and once again the light haired man brushed his lips against hers. Julie's entire body tingled from the soft kiss. She had never before been so turned on from a kiss.

"Oh God," she thought. "I want him to kiss me and touch me until I scream. I need him inside me, right now."

As if he heard her thoughts, he leaned over and gently placed his lips against hers for a third time. An electric current shot through her body and she felt wetness forming between her legs. His tongue gently pried her lips open and thrust into her mouth. The sensation of his tongue touching hers made Julie's legs go weak. Just when she thought her legs would give way completely, the elevator door opened.

The light haired giant took her hand again and led her down the hall. The fifty feet to the hotel room door was a walk of torture for Julie. Her breasts were full and swollen. Her lips were burning

2

from his kiss. Her pussy was dripping wet and screaming with need. He held the door open and followed her inside. She took a step towards the bed but he grabbed her arm, spun her around, and pulled her against his hard muscled chest. He reached behind her, untied her bikini top, and tossed the small piece of red fabric to the floor. He took a moment to caress her hard nipples then moved his big hands lower. In one quick jerk, he ripped the bikini bottoms from her and slid a hand between her legs.

Julie's vision went black as she felt his fingers glide over her clitoris and plunge into her heat and wetness. She put her hands around his neck, feeling a massive orgasm building inside her. Barely able to breath now, she could form only a single thought. She wanted him inside her, now, right now. Her need for him was so bad she thought would die of frustration. Again he seemed to read her thoughts. He picked her up and carried her through the open doors to the balcony.

Feeling the warm ocean breeze and blazing sun on her bare skin, Julie was frantic to free his penis and have him inside her. It didn't matter that it was broad daylight and they were outside. She needed him and would gladly open her body to him anywhere, anytime. He laid her on the expensively cushioned lounger and looked down at her flushed body. His brilliant blue eyes drilled into her and created more heat than she knew was possible. He pulled his swim trunks down, revealing a huge erection. Julie moaned with need as she watched his

3

rock hard penis glide over her stomach and down to her dripping wet pussy.

He was positioned between her legs and poised to enter her when a piercing noise broke the spell. Julie tried to block out the screeching, but it wouldn't go away. She looked up at him, wondering why he didn't silence whatever was causing the awful disturbance. But he wasn't there. Instead, Julie saw her bedroom ceiling, glowing golden from the morning sunlight streaming in. A warm breeze was blowing from the furnace duct. The alarm clock was ringing incessantly, bringing her fully awake.

As she reached to turn off the clock, Julie realized her fingers were wet and slippery. She sighed as reality rushed back at her. The handsome light haired giant had been nothing more than a figment of her sex-starved imagination. The fingers she had felt inside her must have been her own. It has been almost four months since a man had held her, made love to her. Dr. Julie Shelton, thirty years old, blonde, blue eyed, exercise enthusiast, and popular general practitioner in a thriving family practice group. And let's not forget.....dumped on Thanksgiving Day by the man she thought she would spend the rest of her life with....dumped for another woman. The betrayal she felt when Michael had said he was in love with someone else had been horrific and made her feel diminished and unattractive.

What was wrong with her that she couldn't find a decent man to love her and make her feel special and wanted? She knew she had little experience with men. She had spent her college years focusing on getting into medical school and

4

then being in the top of her class once she got there. She had one semi-serious boyfriend in high school, but no one else until she met Michael shortly after she started her residency. He had swept her off her feet and she had never looked back. Never that is until he had dumped her and now she was left wondering what she had done wrong. She certainly didn't want to let another man get that close to her heart but she missed the closeness and intimacy of a lover.

Could that be why this same dream had come to her every night for the last week? Did she unconsciously need someone to make her feel wanted again? Maybe she should take a late February vacation to a warm Caribbean island. She had to do something to get away from the memories and fill the terrible, cold void inside her heart.

"Maybe a warm, sunny beach is just what the doctor should order," she thought as she pushed the covers back and slipped out of bed.

As she headed to the bathroom she wondered if that would even be possible. She had originally scheduled two weeks vacation at the end of February for her honeymoon, a fabulous ski trip to the Swiss Alps. When she had told her medical practice partners that the wedding was off, she had said that she would go ahead and work. They encouraged her to take a vacation anyway. They had deliberately kept her patient load light, advising some time off would be good for her. Maybe they were right. Maybe she should take a few days to try to warm the chill she felt deep in her soul.

"Yes!" she shouted at her sleep-tousled image in the mirror. "Two weeks in the sun and I'll be a new woman!"

All she saw in return was a sleepy, skeptical woman with a determination to make plans anyway.

CHAPTER 2

The last two weeks had flown by and Julie was almost surprised to find herself on an airplane heading to the Cayman Islands in the sparkling Caribbean Sea. Her practice partners had been overly supportive of her plan to go forward with her two-week vacation. Dr. Lincoln, the senior partner, had even commented that maybe some sun would put a little spark in her sad eyes and improve her impatient attitude. At first Julie was offended by his remark, but as she examined her behavior since the infamous Thanksgiving Day dumping, she realized he was right on the mark. She had been testy with her partners and abrupt with some of her more difficult patients.

The flight from Chicago to Miami had been uneventful and now Julie was on the final leg of her trip. Just the sight of the beautiful turquoise water below the plane was beginning to give her a peaceful feeling. As they approached Grand Cayman, the main island of the trio that makes up the Cayman Islands, she began to get restless, ready for her vacation to begin. A short ferry ride from Grand Cayman to Little Cayman and she would be far away from civilization. She chose Little Cayman because of the quiet atmosphere and spectacular beaches. The tour sites on the internet warned that Little Cayman had no nightlife to speak of but that was fine. Julie wasn't feeling up to socializing. All she wanted was sun, sand, surf, and sleep. The plane

7

began to bank to the left and drop down towards the airport.

Three hours and an interesting ferry ride later, Julie was checked into the small oceanfront hotel on Little Cayman. She was unpacked and ready for a light dinner. She dressed in a coral colored sundress that set off her golden hair. Her skin was pale but two weeks of sitting on the beach would bring back the honey brown tan she always sported in the summer. She had asked the desk clerk for a recommendation and was now walking down the beach to The Hungry Iguana restaurant. The sun was dropping down in the west and the sky was a dramatic vista of red, orange, and pink. Julie breathed in the salt-tinged air and immediately felt better. The waves lapping at the beach and the sand under her feet were relaxing her already.

The restaurant was busy with divers, snorkelers, and various other sun bronzed diners. Julie sat alone at a small table on the veranda with a fabulous view of the ocean. It had grown dark while she ate a delicious dinner of fresh fish, grilled vegetables, and a chocolate mousse to die for. As she paid the check, she told the waitress that she would definitely be back again.

"Are you staying here at the Paradise Villas?" the waitress asked.

"No, I'm just down the beach at the Sunset Inn. It's such a cute hotel and I have a balcony that looks directly on the ocean," Julie replied.

"Did you bring a flashlight or lantern for your walk back down the beach?" the waitress asked with concern in her voice.

8

"No, it really didn't dawn on me how dark it would be once the sun went down," Julie replied. "Is there someplace I might buy a flashlight?"

"There's the Village Square beside the old airport terminal that sells all kinds of things including lanterns. They close at six o'clock every evening so it's too late to go there now. There's really no place else close by," the waitress replied.

"No worries," Julie answered. "I'm sure I'll be fine. It's just a short walk directly down the beach. I can almost see the hotel lights from here."

"Be very careful," the waitress warned. "Our quiet little island has been growing since the new airport was built. There are a lot more people here and not all of them are nice ones."

Heeding the waitress' warning, Julie set off down the beach, alert for anything out of the ordinary. She was focused on looking for the lights of her hotel when she stumbled over something.....something that was huge and moving. She screamed and thrashed about, trying to get up off the sand so she could run. She seemed to be totally tangled up in whatever animal it was she had tripped over. Its cold, scaly body was under her legs while its long tail was lashing back and forth. Julie screamed again as she finally got free and began to back away. The big, ugly creature slowly lumbered away from her, headed towards the sawgrass that ringed the edges of the beach.

Walking backwards as she tried to monitor its progress, Julie was completely startled when she bumped into what felt like a concrete wall. She turned around and screamed again when a mountain of a man grabbed her arms. She tried to wrestle free but his big hands held tight.

"Whoa, calm down little lady," the man said in a soft voice. "I'm not going to hurt you and neither is the iguana you stumbled over. As you just saw, we have some of the biggest iguanas on record here on Little Cayman. That one's name is Big Pete and he's one of the biggest iguanas ever recorded. By the way, Big Pete and I both are harmless."

Shaking from back to back frights, Julie took several deep breaths to get her heart rate back to normal. Not only had she just fallen over the biggest iguana ever, but she was now looking up at one of the biggest men she had ever seen. In the dark she could barely make out his face but she didn't need light to tell that he was well over six feet tall, light haired, and built like a weight lifter. His broad shoulders and muscled chest tapered to a narrow waist. She was 5' 8" but next to him she felt tiny, almost like a child.

The man was looking down at her and Julie thought she saw an amused smile on his face. He was laughing at her! She pushed against his massive chest and tried to step back. She got only a few inches when he pulled her back against his chest and kissed the top of her head. His big hands moved slowly up her arms in a soft caress. When he reached her shoulders, his hands glided down her back and cupped her butt. He leaned down and roughly pressed his lips against hers for several seconds. Then he shifted slightly and was again looking at her.

"Don't be in such a hurry to leave Darlin'," he said. "I'm kinda likin' the way you feel pressed up against me. Kinda like the way your lips taste too."

Julie was infuriated that this giant thought he had some kind of right to her body. She was also mortified that her body was suddenly responding to his caresses. She felt her nipples harden and blood rush into her breasts and lower abdomen. Julie shook her head and jerked away from him.

"Who do you think you are and what do you think you're doing?" she demanded as he let go of her.

"I'm Sanders and I think it's pretty obvious that I was holding on to the sweetest, firmest ass I've touched in a very long time," he replied. This time he was definitely smiling at her with that amused look on his face.

"Since we've become so close, I guess you should tell me who you are," he continued.

"Who I am doesn't matter and we are *not* close," Julie answered as she took another step backward.

"Since I saved you from Big Pete, I think maybe you owe me a little something," Sanders said.

"You *saved* me from Big Pete? Are you kidding me? Didn't you just say Big Pete is harmless?" Julie's voice was shaking and her breath was coming in short bursts. "And whether you saved me or not, you have no right to put your hands or lips anywhere on my body. Now if you'll excuse me, I'm leaving."

She stepped around the giant man and headed down the beach. As she stomped away she heard his voice again.

"It was nice meeting you Darlin'. See you tomorrow."

Julie strode headlong down the beach and into her hotel. She didn't look up or stop until she reached her room. She closed the door behind her and leaned back against it trying to calm her breathing. What an arrogant jerk! How dare he touch her like that! How dare he kiss her! As her breathing slowed, Julie became aware that her breasts were swollen and aching for attention. Her lips were bruised from where Sanders had kissed her. And deep inside, she felt an emptiness in her soul that made her want to cry. She took the five steps to the bed, lay face down fully clothed, and began to sob.

CHAPTER 3

"Well now," Sanders mused. "I was absolutely right when I saw her checking in today. That is one fine, firecracker of a woman. Hope I didn't scare her off, but damned if I could help myself. I just had to see what that firm little ass felt like. Mighty fine.....mighty fine."

Sanders chuckled under his breath as he walked back toward the Sunset Inn. As owner and general manager of the hotel, he saw all kinds of people every day. Some very beautiful women had come and gone through those double hardwood doors. Most of the time they were married or with a tour group and he maintained his professional "manager" appearance for them. Oh sure, he had women come on to him from time to time. After all, with his sun bleached hair, blue eyes, and hard body, he was a good-looking man in a rough and tumble kind of way. However, he made it a habit to keep his distance. No reason to give somebody fuel to sue him or his hotel.

This was the first time he remembered such a beautiful, sexy woman staying alone since he opened the hotel six months ago. According to her reservation information, she was a doctor too. He wondered what kind of doctor she was, medical or Ph.D.? It really didn't matter. Either way she had to be intelligent. They didn't hand out the title of doctor to just anyone. Beauty, brains, and single....definitely his kind of woman.

13

It had been a long time since he had actually pursued a woman. When his sexual appetite absolutely had to be filled, he usually went to Grand Cayman and picked up someone in a bar. It was just easier that way and he didn't run the risk of being hurt again. Sometimes he wondered if the intense pain of Susan's betrayal and the subsequent divorce would ever fade away completely. He would never go through that again, never allow someone to get so close! He had been hurt so badly that the only way he had been able to heal was to leave his life in Texas behind. He shook his head and slowly meandered up the path through the dunes toward the hotel's front doors.

Hope my skills haven't gotten too rusty Sanders thought as he strode through the lobby. I could use some good conversation with an intelligent, gorgeous lady followed by some great sex. And if her behavior tonight is any indication, it will be hot, hot, hot sex.

As he circled the reception desk and headed to his personal apartment behind it, he shook his head and cursed himself. What was he thinking anyway? He didn't have time to wine, dine, and converse with anyone, especially a beautiful woman. He had his hands full running this hotel. Any spare time was devoted to the locals and providing for their needs. They had welcomed him and become his new family. With his hotel finished and in business, he was now building his second dream…..a free Medical Clinic for the locals. They worked so hard tending to tourists and asked for so little in return. Sanders had the means to make their lives

14

easier and would do so with the new clinic. He needed to concentrate on the tasks at hand and stop wishing for the moon.

Sanders entered his apartment and poured a strong drink. He needed to clear his head of the gorgeous doctor and refocus his mind. He wandered around the apartment, restless and fidgety. He opened the sliding glass doors to his private terrace. He loved this terrace and had designed it for maximum exposure to the beauty of the island and minimum exposure to prying eyes. He sat in one of the plush lounge chairs and looked out at the amazing night sky.

As Sanders settled himself on his terrace, Julie was dragging herself off the bed two floors directly above his head. Her eyes were red and full of grit from the crying spell. She washed her face, put on a silky nightgown, and started back through the room. That's when she noticed the bottle of wine chilling on top of the small refrigerator. She didn't think it had been there earlier, but she was so tired and depressed now she wasn't sure. Whatever, she thought. It doesn't matter how or when it arrived. It's here and I think I'll have a glass.

She opened the wine, poured a glass, and went out to the surprisingly large balcony. The wine was delicious and the view was breathtaking. As she stood at the balcony railing, Julie could see small waves rushing to the beach, the three-quarter moon rising in the night sky, and more stars than she knew existed. She raised her glass and toasted the universe for the spectacular display it had reserved for her. If anything could get her out of this funk, the beauty of Little Cayman was the perfect medicine.

The wine warmed Julie from the inside out. She drank it quickly and made a fast trip back inside to pour a second glass. Returning to the balcony railing, she thought about the days ahead, days without any planned activities, days with nothing but sun and water. Then her mind drifted back to the man she had run into on the beach.

The Incredible Hulk, Texas style. Texas where everything is bigger, Julie joked to herself and then giggled at the next thought that came to her. Wonder if that applies to all of his body parts?

She allowed her mind to wander a bit and soon realized the second glass of wine was causing her to think some very heated thoughts. Julie drained the wine glass and put it down on the balcony railing. She slowly ran her hands down the front of her nightgown, imagining it was the big Texan touching her. Her nipples were protruding, making her breasts sensitive to the silky fabric rubbing over them. Her breath was coming now in short bursts as a flame began to ignite inside her.

Running her hands down over her stomach, Julie moaned softly as the flame exploded into a raging fire between her legs. She closed her eyes and envisioned Sander's rock hard chest pressing against her back and his big, strong hands sliding down to the hem of her short gown. She felt the silky fabric moving up her thighs to her waist and fingers caressing her belly. The fingers moved slowly down through her trimmed pubic hair and she moaned again as they slid between her legs and across her clitoris. With the wine releasing her inhibitions, Julie stood on the balcony and rubbed her clit until she came….a huge, shuddering orgasm that left her legs weak.

When the spasms finally subsided, Julie realized she had knocked the wine glass off the railing. She had no memory of hearing it shatter below. Too embarrassed by her actions to look over the edge and see where it landed, Julie retreated to her room and collapsed on the bed.

Below, Sanders was looking up at the balcony where he had just witnessed one of the most sensual sights he had ever seen. When her fingers lifted the hem of her gown, his eyes were riveted to the erotic show above him. When they plunged between her legs and she came, his penis throbbed for release too.

The ravishing doctor was obviously letting go and enjoying her stay. With her long blonde hair, full breasts, and very shapely legs, she was amazingly beautiful. To watch her touch her own body with such enjoyment was almost more than he could bear. When she moved back out of his sight, he looked down at the wine glass shattered on the terrazzo tile beside his lounge chair. She must have found the wine he had put in her room while she was at The Hungry Iguana. His eyes moved to the giant erection pulsing beneath his pants. It was going to be a long, frustrating night for the owner of the Sunset Inn.

CHAPTER 4

Julie woke to the sun shining brightly through the sliding glass door. She peeked at the bedside clock to find that it was just a few minutes after six o'clock. Even on vacation her internal clock was waking her up early. She rose and walked out to the balcony to look at the ocean glistening in the sunlight. The water was the most vivid turquoise she had ever seen. It was so clear she could see the dark tops of small coral reefs. She knew from the Internet research she had done back in Chicago that the reefs were teeming with all kinds of fish and exotic sea creatures.

Julie had never been snorkeling but the hotel offered snorkel and scuba lessons according to their website. She thought about it as she stood at the balcony railing and decided to try snorkeling. No way would she try scuba diving however. Julie laughed quietly. She thought of herself as athletic and an exercise buff, but swimming and water sports were things she had long avoided. She could swim well enough to get across the pool and back, but that was about it. She had a huge fear of having her head under water yet here she was in one of the most popular diving areas in the world.

As her eyes scanned the ocean, Julie remembered the wine from the night before and what had happened afterward. She peered cautiously over the railing but didn't see the shattered glass on the terrace below. The occupants of that room must have had it cleaned up already. She was just glad there wasn't anyone sitting down there today. Her red face would have given her away as the culprit if she had been seen looking down.

A short jog on the beach will be the first order of the day Julie thought. Breakfast next followed by a quick trip to that store to get a flashlight. Then the rest of the day can be mine to do nothing but sunbathe.....and maybe snorkel.

Dressing quickly in her jogging shorts, top, and shoes, Julie grabbed her iPod and headed for the beach. She decided to jog the opposite direction from The Hungry Iguana this morning. She didn't know where the irritating Mr. Sanders was staying but she didn't want to run into him again. Although no one else knew of her fantasy last night, she was embarrassed that she had let him wander through her mind that way.

The sky was turning from pale orange to brilliant blue as Julie made her way down the beach. She had never jogged in sand before and was finding it quite a challenge. Her normal five-mile jog would definitely be shortened until she got the hang of it. She was headed directly into the morning sun and felt blinded by the huge yellow ball rising on the horizon. As she pushed and stumbled through the sand, she was concentrating so hard on staying upright that she didn't see the figure jogging toward her. Between the sun in her eyes and the need to watch her footing, Julie ran directly into a massive obstacle. She started to fall backwards, but her arms were grabbed by two huge hands and she was jerked back to her feet.

"Well Darlin', we meet again. People are going to start talking if you keep running into me," Sanders drawled as he gazed quickly up and down the beach. "But today you're in luck....no one on the beach this early except you and me. And I told you I'd see you today."

"Where did you come from?" Julie asked, startled when she realized it was Sanders. "Are you following me?"

"I came from Texas," Sanders replied. "And no, I'm not following you. In case you didn't notice, you ran into me.....again."

"Oh good grief," Julie sighed. "I didn't mean where you live, I meant what are you doing here....no that's not what I meant.....I meant......sheesh, just forget it!"

"How about we start again?" Sanders said, a smile in his blue eyes. "Are you OK? Did you hurt yourself when you stumbled? It takes some time to get used to jogging in the sand. If you've never done it before, you might want to try jogging at the surf line. The sand is packed down a bit more there. Makes for firmer footing when you run."

"Thank you for the information Mr. Know-it-all," Julie said in her most sarcastic voice. "I'll certainly take that under advisement. Now if you will excuse me, I need to finish my run."

Sanders stepped to one side, bowed slightly, and extended an arm up the beach in a gesture of chivalry.

"As you wish madam," he said in a somber tone. "Enjoy the rest of your jog."

Julie brushed past him and headed on up the beach. As she passed, Sanders grinned lewdly and watched her head to the surf line.

Wow that ass looks even better in those skin-tight shorts he thought as he shielded his eyes from the sun. Between the balcony performance last night and this morning's fine looking jog, I need a cold shower before I can get any work done today.

He watched until his eyes were burning and tearing from the bright sunlight. When he could barely see her, he turned and started down the beach. His thoughts were in a whirl over the pretty lady doctor from Chicago.

Julie's head was full of thoughts about Sanders too. She was having trouble concentrating on where her feet were going. All she could think of was his hard, muscular chest and how it felt against her breasts.

"I have to stop thinking about him," she chided herself. "He's arrogant, full of himself, and only looking for a quick romp in the bedroom. So what if he has an amazing muscular build? So what if his deep drawling voice sends shivers down my spine? So what if looking into those eyes makes me weak? I'm done with men!"

At that Julie turned the volume up on her iPod and ran even harder. As the sweat poured from her body, she focused all her attention on keeping her footing in the shifting sand. Finally she turned around and headed back toward the hotel. By the time she reached it, she was drenched in sweat and gasping for breath. The sun was much hotter than she expected and it was quickly draining her.

CAYMAN KISS

Julie stopped at the tiki bar for a quick breakfast and a bottle of water. Sitting at the edge of the beach looking out over the ocean was so spectacular that she knew she was in paradise. Julie drank half the water while she waited for her food. A plate of local fruits and just baked muffins arrived with a glass of fresh squeezed orange juice. She looked up from her plate just as a school of dolphins swam by about a hundred yards out. They were obviously having a good time as they took turns jumping to the delight of Julie and a few other guests who were also early risers.

Although she would have liked to stay and watch longer, she needed to get her shopping done and get to work on her tan. Julie went into the lobby where she made arrangements to rent a bicycle for the duration of her stay. She would use it for her trip to the Village Square, Little Cayman's only shopping site. She ran quickly upstairs to her room, grabbed her small backpack, and stuffed her wallet inside. Back downstairs, she hopped on the bicycle and headed out to shop.

The desk clerk at the hotel had told Julie that it would be about four miles or so via the road winding through the lush tropical foliage. She cycled along the side of the road taking in the beauty of the island. There were so many birds calling that it sounded like a symphony. Julie remembered that this must be the Booby Pond Nature Reserve she had read about and the birds must be the Red-Footed Boobies that came to Little Cayman to breed. The Internet article she read had noted that there was a museum and some sort of house that had an observation deck with telescopes. Maybe I'll check that out later in my trip she thought.

Although the foliage was exquisite, it didn't completely block the merciless sun as it beat down on Julie's head. She made a mental note to buy a hat when she purchased a flashlight at the Village Square. She stopped by the roadside to take a drink from her water bottle. Rummaging through her backpack, she realized she must have left her water at the hotel.

Less than one day on this island and I'm already becoming a laid back, forgetful local, she thought. Well I'll just have to tough it out. Note to self – buy water, hat, and flashlight!

Julie quickly found the shopping center and made her purchases. Her shopping done, Julie got on the bike and headed back to the Sunset Inn. She had a new hat on her head and a sweating bottle of water in her backpack. About halfway back, she found a little shady spot and stopped for a drink. With birds singing around her, she realized she was sweating even more than her water bottle. Must be the humidity she thought.

As she was getting back on the bike she heard something rustling off the side of the road. Before she could get settled on the seat, a giant iguana came lumbering out onto the road fifty feet in front of her. Stifling a scream, Julie watched the big creature move slowly across the road and stop on the centerline. It turned and seemed to look directly at her.

"Alright big boy," Julie said. "I'm going to ride past you and you're going to stay right there. I tangled with your brother Big Pete last night. How about we declare a truce and leave each other alone?"

Julie began to pedal towards the big iguana. He really was an intriguing animal, but that didn't mean she wanted to be friends! As she closed the distance between them, the iguana darted in front of her towards the brush at the side of the road. Startled that he could move that fast, she swerved around him and ended up in a heap in the traffic lane.

"Oh damn!" Julie cried. "That wasn't very nice big boy. I thought we had a truce!"

Hurriedly she picked herself up, not sure whether to laugh because she was talking to iguanas or cry because of the patch of road burn on her right leg. Iguanas two, city doctor zero she thought as she got back on the bike. She hoped the iguanas wouldn't be the death of her vacation.

Julie arrived back at the hotel and put her bikini on. She looked at herself in the mirror before she put on the bright blue cover-up.

"Not bad, not bad at all. Except for the pasty white skin, I look pretty good. Two weeks of beach jogging and sunbathing and I'll be looking really good!" she said as she turned back and forth and posed in front of the mirror. "Now if I just had someone who cared how I look. Oh well, no sense in whining with all that white sand and blue ocean out there."

The hotel offered lounge chairs and umbrellas to their guests. Julie chose one and settled herself for some reading and sunbathing. It was nearing 11:00 o'clock and the brutal sun was high in the sky. She carefully slathered sun screen over all her exposed body parts….at least the ones she could reach. She was wondering how she was going to cover her back when she heard a deep voice.

"Need some help, Darlin'? You don't want to miss any bare skin. The sun will blister skin as beautiful as yours," Sanders drawled.

Julie looked up but with the sun to his back all she could see was a massive outline of a man. However, she knew it was Sanders and that he had a smirk on his face. She leaned forward to say something but before she could open her mouth he had grabbed her bottle of sunscreen.

"Turn around so I can make sure your entire back gets covered," he instructed.

Julie made a huffing noise under her breath and turned sideways on the lounge chair. Sanders sat down beside her and soon his big hands began massaging her back with lotion. Oh God it felt wonderful to have his big hands lightly caressing her shoulders and back. She began to relax as his fingers dug into the tense muscles. They traveled down the center of her back, his thumb rubbing down her spine. He leaned forward, his breath hot on her back and a shiver went through her.

His hands moved further south and she felt his thumbs glide across the small of her back. For Julie, this was a major erogenous zone. A hot, electric pulse shot through her body and she was suddenly aware of a wetness forming between her legs. A small moan escaped her lips. She was floating on a cloud of heat and desire when she felt

25

his fingers slide under the fabric of her bikini bottom. She jolted upright, jerked away, and turned to look at him.

"What do you think you're doing?" Julie asked as her warm bubble burst. "Give me the lotion and go away!"

"Seems to me you were enjoying that quite a bit," Sanders said as he once again looked directly into her eyes. "I know I sure was."

"Please just go and leave me alone. You're obviously staying around here somewhere but I'd be happy if you pretend you don't see me for the rest of your vacation. I'm going to pretend I don't see you. I'm not interested, understand?"

Sanders chuckled. She thought he was a tourist. She obviously didn't realize he owned this hotel and had watched her sensual show last night. Should he enlighten her? Nope, no reason to do that now.

"Enjoy your afternoon. Don't forget to reapply sunscreen even if you're sitting under this umbrella," Sanders replied. "See you again soon."

"Thank you for your concern but I'm a doctor and very aware of sunburn issues and skin cancer concerns. And no, you won't see me again soon."

Sanders stood and his blue eyes pierced hers. That electric frisson passed through her again as she looked deep into his eyes. He stared at her for several moments before he moved. In that short time Julie's blood ran so hot that she was sure she was going to burst into flames.

26

"Have a good afternoon, Darlin'," Sanders croaked.

It was all he could manage. Those few moments when he had stared into her eyes had set his blood on fire too. He wanted her so bad he ached. An image of her standing on the balcony the night before with her fingers between her legs rose before his eyes. Pure desire overcame him. He backed away, almost stumbling into a waiter carrying a tray with a tall, ice cold drink.

That woman is gonna be the death of me, Sanders thought. Another very cold shower is next on my agenda today. I may end up taking more cold showers in the next two weeks than I've ever taken before.

As he started up the path to the hotel he heard the waiter tell Julie that he had her Mai Tai ready.

"Alcohol in this heat? Not smart Dr. Shelton," Sanders grumbled to himself as he went back up the path to the hotel. "But what do I care? You aren't interested, or so you say, so I'll keep my thoughts to myself."

CHAPTER 5

With a start, Julie woke wondering where she was and why it was so hot. It took only a moment to remember she was at the beach and the sun was drilling through the umbrella. She had downed most of her Mai Tai and promptly fallen asleep on her stomach. She rolled over, hoping she hadn't been out too long. In minutes she was dozing again.

Thirty minutes later, Julie woke a second time and finished her now very warm drink. She pulled on the back of the chair until she was sitting up. She was hot and thirsty. Maybe next time that waiter came by she should get some water. She scanned the beach and realized there were quite a few people out now. Many were sunbathing, others were in the water, and there was a group just down the beach apparently getting ready to snorkel.

The snorkel group was being instructed by an extremely good-looking, well built young guy with white blonde hair and a very deep tan. He didn't look a day over eighteen to Julie. She walked to the edge of the water and watched as he showed several people how to adjust their mask and breathing tube. She was extremely hot and sweating profusely now. She walked forward until the water was just above her knees. It was nice and cool, very refreshing.

"Did you want to snorkel too ma'am?" he asked. "The boat will be leaving in about thirty minutes so you still have time to practice with the rest of the group."

"Oh no," Julie stuttered, taken aback that this guy was so young that he called her ma'am. "I'm watching now and trying to cool off a little in the water. Maybe later in the week."

"A pretty lady like you is welcome anytime," the young Adonis replied. "It's a free activity offered by the hotel. You pay nothing unless you want to tip the snorkel instructor."

With that he winked at her and turned around to help a middle-aged lady who was coming out of the water sputtering. Julie walked a little deeper into the ocean, feeling slightly dizzy from the unforgiving sun. Suddenly she was very, very dizzy, and shivering even though she was sweating. Realizing she might be exhibiting signs of heat stroke, she turned to make her way back to the beach. Two steps later the dizziness overtook and she fell into the thigh deep water.

Flailing wildly and choking as she swallowed water, Julie tried desperately to get back to the surface. Even under the water the dizziness was no better and she was shivering uncontrollably. Her brain was racing with thoughts of how she was going to drown in less than three feet of water with dozens of people nearby. It seemed the harder she tried to stand up, the less success she had. Her worst fear was going to be realized. She was going to drown!

Without warning, Julie was suddenly hauled up and out of the water. The sunlight was so bright it stabbed her eyes and she couldn't immediately see who had rescued her. She was coughing and sputtering as she was carried back to the beach. As she was gently laid back on her lounge chair, she realized it was the cute young snorkel instructor. He was looking at her, his face a mask of anxiety.

"Are you OK ma'am? What happened? Can I get you anything?" he asked.

He was a bundle of nerves and tossing non-stop questions at her. People were standing around watching. Julie was totally embarrassed at the ruckus she had caused. What in the world happened out there? Before she could say anything, another wave of chills and dizziness came over her and she started shivering in earnest again. She pulled her big beach towel around her shoulders and looked up at the young instructor.

"I'm not really sure but I think I may have passed out due to the heat," Julie answered. "I was so hot, and then I started chilling and getting dizzy, and the next thing I knew you were pulling me out of the water. Thank you so much! I could have died out there without you."

"Well, that's part of my job," he said in a much calmer voice. "Glad to be of help."

"A job you better get back to, Skip," Sanders said as he pushed through the crowd.

"Uh yes sir, no problem Mr. Sanders. I think she's OK but she may have heat stroke," Skip replied as he began backing away.

"Who do you think you are anyway? God?" Julie was aggravated that Sanders was there once again. "You have no right to boss hotel employees around. That young guy saved my life and before I can properly thank him, you have the nerve to dismiss him!"

30

"I'm not God, Dr. Shelton. Not by a long shot. But since I am his boss, I think it's ok for me to send him back to do what I'm paying him to do." Sanders replied.

"You're his boss?" Julia asked in confusion. "I thought the hotel offered the snorkel lessons."

"The hotel does offer the snorkel lessons and since I own the hotel, I guess that makes me his boss," Sanders answered with a sly grin playing across his face. "Kind of makes me the boss of pretty much everyone in the hotel except the guests."

"You own the Sunset Inn? What does that mean?" Julie was really confused now.

"I'm sole owner of the Sunset Inn, general manager, and the person who makes sure all of my guests are treated very well," Sanders continued. "And since you're obviously having some issues with the sun, it's my responsibility to get you back up to your room."

"Not necessary," Julie stated emphatically. "I'm perfectly capable of getting myself up to my room, thank you."

"Yes, it is necessary," Sanders said as he offered his hand to her. "Let me help you up from the chair and I'll take you up to your room where it's air conditioned. I take my responsibility to my guests very seriously."

"As I said, it's not necessary. I can make it by myself." Julie asserted.

She was very irritated with herself and with the obnoxious Mr. Sanders. Julie batted his hand away and stood up. She was immediately assailed by a wave of dizziness and sat back down. She looked up to see Sanders trying hard to contain a smirk that was playing across his face.

"Oh yeah, you're definitely gonna make it by yourself," he drawled. "Look, quit playing the independent female and let me carry you up to your room. The sun down here is intense, you obviously have heat stroke, and you need air conditioning and lots of fluids."

"I know what I need," Julie snapped back at him. "I'm a doctor. As in MD, medical doctor. I realize I didn't drink enough water for the time I was outside so I'm dehydrated. Give me a bottle of water and a few minutes and I'll be fine. I can make it back to my room under my own power."

"Dr. Shelton, I am responsible for all of my guests. I take it very seriously when one of them falls sick. Now you have two options. One, you can let me carry you up to your room in a modest fashion. Or two, I will pick you up, throw you over my shoulder like a sack of potatoes, and take you to your room that way. You can choose how you want to go through the lobby of *my* hotel but it won't be under your own power. So?" Sanders stood looking down at her, his face hardened with irritation at her unreasonable attitude.

Fuming at this insane man but understanding how weak she was, Julie quietly agreed to let him carry her. He reached down and very gently scooped her up in his massive arms. Without thinking, she put her arms around his neck and laid her head on his shoulder. It felt good, too good.

"Alex," Sanders said addressing the waiter who was standing in the crowd watching. "Can you gather Dr. Shelton's things and have someone bring them to her room along with several bottles of ice cold water? She's in room 304."

"Sure thing Mr. Sanders," Alex replied. "I'll be there in a few minutes. Anything else you need, sir?"

"One more thing. Under no circumstances is Dr. Shelton to have any more alcohol today. Understood?" Sander questioned.

"Understood!" Alex was nodding his head and grinning.

Ready to object to Sanders issuing orders about what she could or could not have, Julie opened her mouth to speak when another wave of dizziness and chills washed over her. She began to shiver uncontrollably again despite the towel around her shoulders. She closed her mouth and burrowed deeper into Sanders' shoulder.

"Yeah, you're definitely not OK," Sanders murmured into her hair. "Let's get you inside and get some liquids into you."

Each step was torture for Sanders as he walked up the path through the dunes, into the hotel, and across the lobby. Having this exquisitely enticing creature nestled against him was almost more than he could bear. Knowing what was underneath the towel made it even more difficult to think straight. What in the world had possessed him to come running down from the lobby when he had seen her fall into the water? Skip had received lifeguard training as well as CPR instruction as part of his orientation. He required every employee to be certified, no matter what their duties were. Any one of them could have taken care of this.

Finally reaching the door to her room, Sanders shifted Julie in his arms so he could reach the master key card he always carried. The towel fell from her shoulders and his hand was unexpectedly caressing bare skin. Groaning aloud, he pulled the key card from his pocket, slipped it into the slot, and pushed the door open.

"If I'm that heavy, put me down. I'm sure I can make it from here," Julie growled.

She didn't realize that the groan had been his reaction to feeling her soft skin under his hand, smelling her fragrant blonde hair, and the sudden vision he had of her on the balcony of this very room last night. He removed his hand and she slid slowly down the front of him.

Oh God he thought as an erection began to bulge under his pants. I have to have her.

Julie slipped into the room and leaned against the open door, her own thoughts in turmoil. This man was making her crazy. He was arrogant, over bearing, irritating, and she wanted him so badly she could barely breathe. She had felt his erection as her hips slid down the front of his pants. The heat stroke must be worse than she thought.....she was getting extremely aroused knowing that he clearly wanted her too.

"Mr. Sanders, thank you for getting me safely to my room," she said in her most formal tone. She had to get him out of there and fast. "I can take it from here. I appreciate your help but I'm OK now."

"No problem, Darlin'," Sanders drawled, standing awkwardly at the door. He wasn't sure he could walk with his penis standing straight up at attention. "Alex will be here with water. Make sure you drink plenty this afternoon. I'll send a dinner tray up later this evening, on the house. Just call the front desk when you're ready to eat."

"Thank you again. I have it under control now. I'll drink plenty of water and rest up until tomorrow. Goodbye," she said hurriedly, wishing to close the door without appearing ungracious.

Julie was anxious for him to be gone so she could get in bed and pull the covers over her head. What kind of a doctor was she that she had not heeded the signs of heat stroke this afternoon? Plus she was embarrassed that her body was reacting to him in such a strong way. She started to shut the door but he put his big hand against it. She looked at the hand and remembered how it felt caressing her skin. Her knees were weak again but not from heat stroke this time.

"If you need anything tonight, call the front desk," he replied. "Like I said, I take my responsibility to my guests seriously. I'm here....uh, the hotel staff is here to help you anyway we can. Don't forget to call for dinner."

Sanders stepped back and watched as she closed and locked the door. If she hadn't been so weak, he might have forced things and tried to kiss her. Her body showed the unmistakable signs of arousal even though her words said something different. He wondered what she would have done had he simply reached out and run his fingers over

35

her hard nipples. Then he wondered what she would have done if he had thrown her on the bed and removed the two tiny scraps of fabric covering that luscious body. Realizing that he was still staring at her closed door, Sanders turned and strode toward the elevator. Oh yes, he was definitely going to need an ice cold shower.

On the other side of the door, Julie was having similar thoughts. She almost wished he had held on to her and carried her to the bed. In her mind she could see his big hands covering her breasts, caressing, squeezing…oh God. Then they were replaced by his mouth licking and sucking on her nipples. She moaned and in her mind saw herself open her legs to him, wanting him, needing him. Her daydream was shattered by a loud knock on the door she was still leaning against.

"Dr. Shelton? Are you ok?" an alarmed voice asked.

It was Alex with her things. Julie opened the door, assured the waiter she was fine, and took her beach bag and the tray with bottled water. She moved back into the room, put on some comfortable pajamas, and settled onto the couch to replenish her fluid levels. The doctor part of her mind took over as she calculated how much water she needed to drink.

Loud knocking woke Julie several hours later. She looked at the clock and realized that after drinking two bottles of water, she had fallen asleep for over six hours. Heat stroke had taken a greater toll than she realized. As she rose from the couch, the knocking grew more insistent.

"Be right there! Hold on a minute," Julie called out.

She stopped quickly in the bathroom and splashed water on her face. A glance in the mirror told her it was hopeless. Her face was slightly sunburned, her hair was a mess from sleeping on the couch, and her eyes were ringed with dark circles. Oh well, no one here she wanted to impress anyway. Looking through the peephole on the door, Julie saw Sanders standing outside. She sighed, too tired for another round of aggravation from him. She opened the door and stood in the doorway, subtly telling him he was not welcome.

"Mr. Sanders, what can I do for you?" she asked.

"Katie, the evening desk clerk, said you never called down for dinner. It's after 9:00 so I was a little worried. Thought I should bring you a tray and make sure you're OK," Sanders replied.

"I'm surprised you're still on site," Julie countered. "I would have thought you would be at home with your loved ones by now."

"Home is an apartment behind the registration desk. It's actually on the ground floor, directly below your room," Sanders said. "I told the staff to let me know when, I mean if, they heard from you. It's really none of your business but I live alone. My family, at least what's left of it, is all in Texas."

Hearing the sadness in his voice, Julie softened slightly. There was a hurt tone that she could definitely identify with. It was the sound of someone betrayed by a lover. She opened the door wider, stepped back, and invited him in. Sanders put the tray of food down on the table, turned on some lights, and then looked at her. She looked absolutely delectable in soft, silky pajamas with her hair mussed from sleeping. He hoped he wasn't making a mistake being in this room with her.

"Sit down and eat," he said softly. "You need some fuel so your body can recover from the heatstroke."

Heeding his advice, Julie sat at the table and ate delicious seafood salad with homemade rolls. She was conscious of Sanders watching her every move. And she was conscious that her body was flushing all over as his gaze heated her blood. Finished with the fabulous meal, she rose from the chair and walked toward the couch where he sat. Halfway across the room, she felt dizzy again and began to shake. She grabbed the edge of the dresser to steady herself. Sanders was up in a flash and beside her before she knew it.

"What's wrong? Are you still dizzy?" he asked his voice full of concern.

"Yes a little bit. I guess I seriously underestimated the effects of the sun down here and the heat stroke is worse than I thought. We don't see much of that in Chicago," she answered.

"Let's get you into bed. Looks like you were sleeping on the couch before. You'll rest better in the bed," Sanders said guiding her to the king sized bed with it's view of the ocean. "I'll just stay here on the couch for awhile until I'm sure you're alright."

"No, absolutely not," Julie said in a weak voice. "I'll be just fine once I get more sleep."

"I'll get no sleep at all if I don't know that you're OK." Sanders was adamant. "I'll be right here on the couch if you need anything. No sense in arguing because I'm not changing my mind. Now get in bed and rest."

Afraid he would pick her up again and set of those crazy feelings, Julie slid onto the bed and under the covers. Sanders busied himself with turning off lights and finding a spare pillow in the closet. Once he was settled on the couch, the room grew silent.

"Thank you for everything Mr. Sanders," Julie said quietly. "I may not have shown it, but I do appreciate your concern."

"It's no problem, Dr. Shelton," he replied.

"I guess if you're sleeping on my couch you should call me Julie," she whispered.

"OK Julie. My first name is Simon but everyone calls me Sanders," Sanders chuckled at first but then his voice got soft. "Simon was my dad. He passed away when I was a teenager and I never really felt like I could fill his shoes."

There it was again, that sad tone of voice. The voice of someone deeply hurt. Could this irritating, aggravating man actually have a soft side? Julie was thinking about that when she fell deeply asleep.

Several hours later she came fully awake as the room lit up followed by a huge crashing noise. Within seconds, another streak of lightening flashed, then there was a huge popping sound followed by

thunder so loud it shook the sliding glass door. Julie
screamed, disoriented by the savage power of the
storm outside her window. Before the scream died,
Sanders was at her side, folding her in his arms.

"It's okay, Darlin'. Just a storm, it will be
alright," Sanders crooned softly in her ear. "I'm here
and I'll never leave you."

Feeling safer than ever before in his arms,
Julie leaned her head back. Another flash of
lightening lit the room and she could see Sanders
looking down at her. His eyes mirrored the wild
desire she was sure he could see in her eyes. He
leaned down and tentatively placed his lips on hers.
A sigh escaped from her and he deepened the kiss,
sliding his tongue into her mouth. She was on fire
now, his kisses so sensual. Another crash of thunder
and his arms went tightly around her, pressing her
hard against his chest.

He continued to kiss her lips, her face, her
ears, her neck, until her body was humming with
need. One hand slipped under her pajama top and
she gasped as his fingers brushed her nipple. She
felt both nipples harden and her breasts began to
swell. He pushed the shirt up and over her head,
freeing her perfect breasts for his lips to explore. His
head moved down and he took one nipple into his
mouth, sucking lightly until she was gasping for
breath. His hands pushed her gently back on the bed
and he released her nipple from his mouth.

Sanders' hands reached down and slipped
Julie's pajama bottoms down over her hips, dropping
them to the floor when they reached the end of her
long, gorgeous legs. He ran his hands over her

stomach, down her legs, and then back up again to the V between her legs. He loved the softness of her skin, the scent of her arousal. His hands easily spread her legs and he moved between them. His tongue slid between her pussy lips and flicked her sensitive swollen clitoris. She moaned and tensed and he began licking her feverishly. She was so wet…much wetter than he had expected. He slid two fingers in her and she arched up, a long low moan escaping from her mouth. His fingers began sliding in and out of her while his tongue continued to tease her. She grabbed the sheets as her body rocked to the rhythm of his fingers and tongue.

In minutes Julie screamed as she experienced the most amazing, shattering orgasm of her life. There was no thought, nothing but the incredible spasms inside her. She rode a wave of pleasure she didn't know was possible. When it started to subside, Sanders began licking and fingering her until she was once again at a pinnacle of pleasure she had only dreamed of. Again and again and again he brought her to orgasm, until finally she could take no more. She panted out a plea to stop and he slid up her body until he was fully on top her.

Sanders kissed her and Julie tasted herself on his tongue. His hands seemed to be all over her body, enflaming her with desire yet again. She could feel his erection pressing against her leg. Oh God she needed him, needed him inside her, stroking her. As if he could read her mind, he gently spread her legs with one knee and slid his hard, pulsing penis into her. He groaned, his penis enveloped in her heat and wetness, her pussy tight around him. He began

41

to move inside her, slowly at first, then faster and faster.

He stroked her again and again with his hard shaft, his mind focused on nothing but her moans and the feeling of being inside her. Her legs instinctively spread wider and his penis went deeper and deeper into her. She was moaning non-stop now, her eyes squeezed tightly shut, her orgasm building and building. His rhythm never let up until she screamed one last time, her pussy tightening around him. He pushed deeper into her and groaned. He was lost, he knew it deep in his soul. One final stroke and his hot juices gushed into her, his orgasm so intense he thought he might pass out. He collapsed on top of her, both of them trying to regain their breath. Finally he rolled off and pulled her to him. His arm around her shoulders, his legs tangled in hers. She sighed a soft goodnight and was asleep in minutes. He lay for a long time wondering what he had gotten himself into before he too succumbed to the stress of the day.

CHAPTER 6

It was warm and sunny as she lay on the beach but what was that awful noise? Looking around, Julie realized she was alone on the most beautiful beach she had ever seen and the thumping sound was getting louder. What in the world was going on? She jumped up from the lounge chair and scanned the horizon, very confused. How did she get to this primitive, unspoiled paradise? She closed her eyes trying to remember and when she opened them again, she was in her hotel room.

Julie sat up in bed, realizing she had been dreaming again but she could still hear the loud thumping. As she slipped out of the tangled sheets, she saw a helicopter rise from the beach and head away from the island. She ran to the balcony and looked out at the ocean as it disappeared from sight.

Oh my God, what have I done, she thought as the night before came rushing back to her. Did I really invite him into my bed last night? And where is he this morning?

The slight soreness between her legs confirmed that she had indeed invited him in and the rising heat she felt told her she had enjoyed it immensely. She didn't know whether to be annoyed or happy that for once in her life her body had overruled her mind. But she was definitely annoyed that he had stolen out of her room in the early morning without so much as a goodbye. She glanced down at the patio directly below her balcony and felt her face go red. What was it he had said?

Something about his personal apartment being behind the reception desk and directly below her room.

"Oh no!" Julie cried as recognition dawned. "My wine glass shattered on his personal patio. Please don't tell me he was sitting there when...."

But she couldn't say it, couldn't even think that he had seen her that first night. Chiding herself for being weak and foolish, she sat down on the lounge chair as she experienced a slight wave of dizziness. Hoping this wave was from hunger, Julie decided to go down to the tiki hut and see if she could get some breakfast. She went back into the room and glanced at the clock on her way to the bathroom. It was already eleven o'clock! She couldn't remember the last time she had slept this late. Something about island life was really relaxing her.

"Island life?" Julie snorted. "I don't think so! Heat stroke combined with the best sex I've ever had in my life is more like it. But what do I do now? Probably nothing since he left before I woke up. I guess I had my first one night stand."

Still unsure of her next step with Sanders, Julie showered, put on a sundress, and went downstairs. As she strolled through the lobby, she noticed small groups of hotel employees standing in knots, looking anxious, and talking quietly. She wondered what that was all about but hunger overtook her curiosity. She went through the massive wooden doors and down the path toward the oceanside tiki hut. She loved that the hotel's small

restaurant was under the tiki hut's roof and included
an amazing view of the ocean.

Julie found an open table and looked over the
menu. It contained a limited selection of items but
each capitalized on the fresh seafood and exotic
tropical fruits readily available in the Caribbean.
Fresh baked goods were also prevalent since the
hotel made all of their own breads and desserts.
Deciding on fresh baked pineapple bread, grilled
shrimp, and fruit, Julie looked up to see a familiar
waiter approaching.

"Dr. Shelton, how are you today?" Alex
exclaimed. "I hope you're feeling better!"

"Much better Alex, thank you," Julie replied,
smiling at the young man. "I drank lots of water and
got a good night's sleep. I'm ready for another day
in paradise."

"Glad to hear it," Alex said. "What can I get
you today?"

Julie placed her order and sat back to wait.
She looked out over the water as she waited, awed
once again at how clear and blue it was. With the
sun reflecting on it, the ocean looked like it was
covered in diamonds. Little Cayman had to be the
most restful, peaceful place on earth she thought as a
flock of birds made a graceful arc in the sky and flew
inland. Red-footed boobies for sure....they were
everywhere. This would be a fabulous spot for a
honeymoon she thought, then shook her head. She
had to rid herself of thoughts of Michael and his
betrayal.

"Oh no, not going there today. Time to move
on," she said to herself. "Maybe it doesn't have to

be a one night stand with Sanders. Maybe it can be a vacation fling. But maybe he's not interested in more. After all, he left without a word....last night.....this morning....I don't even know when he left!"

Her reverie was broken when Alex arrived with her food. He set the plate of shrimp and fruit in front of her and placed a carafe of fresh orange juice and a basket of warm bread on the table. The aroma of freshly baked bread and succulent grilled shrimp made Julie's mouth water.

"Wow, this looks and smells wonderful," she pronounced. "I can't wait to dig in. I'm starving!"

"You waited just long enough after this morning's commotion Dr. Shelton," Alex responded. "We finished cleaning sand off all the tables about ten minutes ago. The helicopter really kicked up quite a sand storm but that's okay if it means Skip will get good treatment at the hospital on the big island."

"I'm sorry," Julie said. "I must have missed something. Are you talking about Skip who does the snorkel lessons? Why did he need to go to the hospital?"

"Skip didn't come in to work today." Alex's voice was quiet but rushed. "He wasn't answering his cell phone either so Mr. Sanders went to look for him. Skip is never late, never misses a day of work, so of course everybody was worried. Mr. Sanders found him unconscious by the side of the road not far from the little house he lives in. His bicycle was in the ditch, mangled and twisted like he had been hit by a car. His pants pockets were pulled out and

46

empty, all of his tips from yesterday were gone. It looks like those robbers struck again. Mr. Sanders had the ambulance bring him here and got a helicopter from the big island to come and get him. Then he went with Skip in the helicopter."

"Oh no!" Julie was stunned. "Skip saved my life yesterday. If it hadn't been for him, I would have drowned when I passed out in the water. I'm so sorry for him. But why would they take him to Grand Cayman? Was he so badly hurt that the local doctor and hospital couldn't take care of him?"

"All we have here are the island EMTs. They took one look at Skip and told Mr. Sanders that he needed a hospital. We don't have a doctor yet but hopefully we'll get one when they finish the new Medical Center. Mr. Sanders said he would do everything possible to recruit a doctor to be on staff there," Alex replied.

"Oh," Julie replied, flabbergasted. "No doctor or hospital? I had no idea there were no medical facilities on the island."

"There will be soon," Alex went on. "That's what I was trying to say. Mr. Sanders is building a medical clinic for us. He'll be looking for a doctor soon so everything will be ready to go when the building is finished."

Alex scanned the tables and then looked back at Julie.

"I need to run. Table six is waving at me. Do you need anything else?"

"Can you ask Mr. Sanders or someone on staff to let me know how Skip is doing, please?" Julie asked. "I'd really like to see him before I go home. I owe him such a debt that I'd be happy to help him anyway I can."

"Not to worry, Dr. Shelton," Alex said. "Mr. Sanders gave specific orders that we were to watch out for you today. He said he would check up on you when he gets back. You can find out directly from him how Skip is and if he needs anything."

"Thank you, Alex," Julie responded tensely. "I guess I better get busy on this delicious looking meal."

Alex walked away leaving Julie seething inside. Who did that arrogant jerk Sanders think he was, telling his staff to watch out for her? She was livid that he thought she needed to be watched over like some kind of misdirected child. She put her fork down and took several calming breaths. When she started eating again, she silently admitted that it felt nice to know someone cared if she was all right. As she ate, her mind drifted back to last night and how safe she felt in his arms. It suddenly dawned on her that he probably left her bed because Skip was missing. Well, maybe there was hope for a vacation fling after all!

Julie finished her lunch and wandered toward to the hotel. She had decided to keep things low key today and went back up to her room. Several hours passed as she sat reading on her balcony. Late in the afternoon she took her Kindle and a bottle of water downstairs and found a comfortable chair by the now shaded pool. She was still sitting there when Sanders strode up.

"Hi Darlin'," Sanders said. "How are you feeling?"

Julie looked up at him and felt an immediate flash of electricity go through her body. She instantly remembered how it felt when first his fingers and then his swollen penis entered her. She felt her entire body flush as she looked deep into his blue eyes.

"I feel great. Spent the day relaxing and resting," she replied. "How's Skip? I've been worried about him all afternoon."

"Skip will be okay. He needs a little recovery time but he should get full use of his leg back with some therapy," Sanders declared.

"What happened to his leg?" Julie asked. "I heard he was likely hit by a car and robbed. It sounded like his injuries were pretty severe."

"I'm tired, sweaty, and starved," Sanders answered. "Why don't you join me for dinner and I'll tell you what happened. We can eat on my terrace. It has the best view from anywhere on the property."

Julie hesitated but then decided what the heck. She was hungry and desperately wanted to be sure the boy who had saved her life was going to be okay. She was also a little curious whether Sanders would try for a repeat of last night's performance.

"Sounds good," she said. "Let me go up to my room and freshen up. I'm not very comfortable having dinner in my bathing suit."

"Why don't you meet me at the reception desk in thirty minutes? I'll order some dinner and get a shower while you're changing."

Thirty minutes later, Julie was dressed in a silky, aqua colored sundress, her blonde hair held up

49

off her neck with a silver starburst clip. Around her neck was a delicate silver chain holding a tiny seahorse that nestled between her breasts. She took the steps down to the first floor and as she crossed the lobby she was aware that Sanders' eyes followed her every move. The dress clung to her curves and she knew she looked good in it. He came out from behind the reception desk and walked toward her.

"Beautiful" was all he said as he looked her up and down. His eyes stopped as he caught a flash of light glinting off the diamond chip that served as the seahorse's tiny eye. He silently wished he could take its place and forever be between those amazing breasts. He took her hand in his and led her down a side hallway. The heat from the contact sent that electric jolt through Julie once again. Oh God, she wanted him so bad her knees were weak.

Sanders put a key card into the slot on an unmarked door and they entered the foyer of his apartment. As soon as they entered the living room, he spun her around and pulled her to him. He held her close and gently touched his lips to hers. A fire ignited in Julie and she strained upward to press herself tight against him, her tongue sliding between his lips. They both groaned as the kiss deepened and heat engulfed their bodies. His hands slid down to her butt and stayed there, caressing her firm round ass through the silky material. He was certain if she had any panties on at all, it had to be the tiniest thong known to man. He now knew what heaven was like.

Sanders was lost in a giant wave of desire. He was rock hard in seconds, his erection pressing against her belly. His only thought was of removing

50

her dress and feasting his eyes on her full breasts and that tiny thong. He pulled the dress up in the back and ran his big hands over her naked butt. Her butt cheeks were as firm and round as he remembered from last night with just a teeny tiny slip of material running between them. He wanted to lay her face down on the bed and lick every inch of that enticing ass and those long, perfect legs, then roll her over and lick and suck her luscious breasts.

Julie suddenly pulled away and Sanders realized someone was knocking on his door. Grumbling low in his throat, he released her and pulled his white button down shirt out of his pants to cover the bulge in his pants. He went to the door and admitted a hotel staff member with a small dining cart. The cart was pushed into the dining area and the table set in short order. The staff member quickly withdrew after asking his boss if they needed anything else.

"Well, I guess we better eat while it's hot," Julie stammered, her heart beating wildly from his caresses. "It smells wonderful."

"Not as good as you smell," Sanders whispered. "But Miss Marie, my Cayman cook, will have my hide if I send the tray back with any food on it. It's her personal mission to make me as fat as Big Pete, your iguana friend."

Sanders moved nervously around the table, helping Julie with her chair and putting the serving dishes out. He then busied himself with opening a bottle of wine and filling two wine glasses. Julie looked under the lids of the serving dishes to find a thick slab of fish grilled to perfection, rice flecked with red peppers and mango, and a mound of salad greens. The bread basket was filled with a variety of still warm breads wrapped in a cloth napkin.

"May I propose a toast to the most beautiful woman on this island?" Sanders asked staring straight into her eyes. "And thank you for joining me tonight. It's a pleasure to have such mesmerizing company at dinner."

"Thank you for inviting me," Julie replied feeling his eyes looking into her soul. "I'm sure you have beautiful, mesmerizing women at your table all the time."

"Actually, you're the first woman I've ever invited into my personal space. I don't entertain much and have no family here," he answered, still holding her eyes captive with his.

In that moment, Julie knew he was telling the truth. She could see it in his eyes, hear it in the sad tone of voice. She wondered who had wounded this man so deeply that he had left everything behind and banished himself to this far away island. She told herself that it didn't matter, it was only a vacation fling. But in her heart, it did matter and she didn't know what to do about it.

There was a short, awkward silence as they looked at each other. Then Sanders broke eye contact and they began to eat. The food was delicious and the wine was outstanding. When a second glass was poured, Julie recognized the bottle as the kind of wine that had been left in her room the first night.

"I love this wine," she commented. "Please thank whoever on your staff left me a bottle the other day."

"You're welcome." Sanders nodded at her.

"Um, okay." Julie said in confusion. Then it hit her. "You left the wine in my room?"

"Yes," he responded. "I saw you checking in and thought you were the most alluring woman I had ever seen. I thought a woman that beautiful deserves the best we have to offer so I put a bottle of wine from my personal stock in your room while you were out to dinner. I hope you enjoyed it."

"Yes, yes I did," she stammered.

Julie was flustered. She was remembering what she had done on the balcony after she had two glasses of this same wine the other night. Now she was wondering if he knew the broken wine glass was hers, or worse, if he had seen her. This conversation could rapidly become embarrassing.

Sanders flashed a secret smile at her, as if he was reading her mind. He stared into her eyes once again and her entire body went white hot. He rose from the table and walked behind her chair. His hands lightly grazed her shoulders and she was sure she heard him sigh. He reached down to pull her chair out, leaning over to brush his lips across the top of her head in the process. Julie rose as he pulled her chair back. She picked up her wine glass and moved away, nervous with desire for him.

"Let's take our wine out on the terrace," Sanders suggested. "We can look at the stars while we finish it."

They walked through the sliding glass doors and Julie's jaw dropped when she saw the view he had of the black ocean and the millions of stars in the sky. The half moon seemed so much bigger than it did in Chicago. She was absolutely dazzled by the beauty of the stars in the endless night sky.

Sanders came up behind her and put his free arm around her, pulling her against his chest. She could feel his heart beating against her back and her own heart was ready to burst out of her chest. They stood like that for several long minutes, slowly drinking the wine. They were both feeling the incredible sexual attraction between them as they gazed at the heavens.

When the wine was gone, Sanders took both glasses and set them on the patio table. He turned back to look at Julie and was struck again by her beauty and innate sensual nature. He took her by the hand and led her to the lounge chair he had been sitting on that first night...the night that he watched her touching herself. He sat down and pulled her down onto his lap. He was kissing her neck and seemed to be breathing in her scent while his hand found its way up her thigh. He leaned back and watched her face as his hand reached the tiny scrap of fabric that made up her thong panties.

"Oooooh God," Julie moaned when he touched her swollen, sensitive clit through the fabric.

Sanders continued to slide his fingers across the silky material and tease her, making her moan and grab his shoulder to stay upright on his lap. He was enjoying watching the expressions on her face change while his fingers sent waves of pleasure through her body. This was the part he had missed the other night and the whole picture was the most erotic vision he had ever seen. Finally he slipped his fingers under the thong and plunged them into her wetness. She stiffened, put her arms around his neck, and cried out as an enormous orgasm overtook her.

"You're so beautiful when you come," he whispered in her ear as she fell against his shoulder. "I knew when I saw you on the balcony the other night that your face would be as expressive as the rest of your body."

"What? You saw me?" Julie pulled away to look at him. Her face was bright red with embarrassment.

" I was sitting here when a wine glass came crashing down beside me," Sanders began as Julie turned her face away. "When I looked up I saw the most sensual woman I could ever imagine standing in the moonlight, touching herself. I can't get that picture out of my mind, it comes to me in dreams at night."

"You spied on me?" she shouted as she attempted to get off his lap.

Sanders held Julie tight as she struggled to get up. He could see that she was extremely uncomfortable with his confession but he had to make her understand that there was no shame in what she had done. He had to let her know what a sexy, desirable woman she was.

"I didn't spy," he said. "I looked to see where the glass came from and saw you standing there.

You were beautiful, exotic looking, and watching you was the ultimate sensual experience for me."

"Oh my God," Julie groaned and all the fight went out of her. "I…I….I…..oh God…." And she hung her head, too upset to look at him.

"Darlin', don't look like that." Sanders grabbed her chin and tilted her head up to make her look at him. "Don't you get it? There's nothing for you to be embarrassed or ashamed about. You're an amazing, incredibly sensual woman and what I saw the other night was the most erotic thing I have ever seen a woman do. Thinking about it makes me insane with need. Do you know how many cold showers I've had to take in the last few days?"

Julie smiled shyly, unsure if he was being serious. He kissed her ear and murmured that it was alright, she was beautiful and sexy and he wanted her to be free with her sexuality, to do whatever felt good to her.

"Honestly?" she asked. "You want me to do whatever feels good?"

"Of course," Sanders replied. "That's what sex should be all about….feeling good, enjoying each other to the fullest."

Julie stood and pulled him up to his feet. She released her hair from the silver clip, pulled his head down close to her face and kissed him with all the passion and heat she had coursing through her body. When she pulled away, Sanders realized she had unzipped his pants and they had fallen around his feet. She pushed him back down on the lounge chair, put a pillow on the tile floor, and knelt down between his legs. She took his already hard penis in

56

her hand and began to lick it with her hot, wet tongue. She licked his balls, up the hard shaft, circled the head with the tip of her tongue, and then licked back down. Sanders groaned as she tightened her grip on him and stroked up and down with her hand over and over and over. When he thought he could stand no more, she leaned over and took him into her mouth, sucking and licking until he was crazed with the need to explode, the need to be inside her.

Sanders reached down and pulled Julie's dress up to her neck. She released his penis from her mouth as the dress was pulled off over her head. He caught a glimpse of her full breasts and hard nipples before she leaned back over his penis. He had to have her, now, right now.

"Stand up, let me look at you," he told her, his hands caressing her hips and sliding her thong down as she stood. "God you're the hottest, most sexual woman I've ever known. I need to be inside you. I need to feel your heat wrapped around me."

He stood, then picked her up and she instinctively wrapped her legs around him. He pushed his purple, throbbing penis into her, feeling her muscles tighten around him. She threw her head back, pressing her swollen breasts into his chest and pushing him deeper into her dripping wet pussy. He had taken only two steps across the terrace, when she came the first time, clutching him around the neck while he tried to maintain his balance. Another four steps and he had to stop again while another orgasm rocked her. Every few steps she went into spasms of pleasure.

Finally he reached the bedroom and laid her gently on the bed while she gulped air, trying to calm her breathing. He watched her face for a few moments but he couldn't wait any longer. He had to be inside her, had to stroke her to another mind blowing orgasm. He moved between her legs and very, very slowly slid into her. She moaned with each small thrust until he began to lose control. His thrusting became faster and her moans turned into a single cry as she began coming non-stop. He was again watching her face when she cried out very loud and he pushed as deep into her as possible. She screamed as she crashed over the edge and he was lost, groaning and gushing hot cum into her.

Sanders collapsed on top of her, totally spent and unable to move. When his breathing slowed, he rolled off and pulled her onto his chest. He needed to hold her, to feel her breath on his skin. They lay entwined until their eyes were heavy and their exhausted bodies were ready to let go of the day. As her eyes fell shut, Julie remembered that they hadn't discussed what had happened to Skip. Tomorrow, she thought, tomorrow.

CHAPTER 7

Julie woke to the competing aromas of coffee and hot bread. She opened her eyes to an unfamiliar bedroom and was slightly disoriented until she remembered the evening before....dinner with Sanders, kneeling before him on the terrace, the walk from the terrace to this bed. She had never known that a man and woman could experience such heat and electricity. And then in the middle of the night she had wakened to what she first thought was a dream. Very soon she realized it wasn't a dream at all....it was Sanders sucking on her nipples, touching her, sliding his hardness into her.....and she had been taken to those dizzying heights all over again.

"Hey sleeping beauty," Sanders whispered as he came into the room and sat on the edge of the bed. "You're so sexy with your hair wild and your eyes still drowsy looking. God I wish I could climb back in there with you. I can think of a thousand ways to make love to you right now."

Feeling wanton, Julie slid over in the bed, looked at him with passion in her eyes, and pulled the cover back in invitation. Sanders feasted his eyes on her magnificent body. He reached over and ran his big hand over her stomach, down to her pubic hair. He groaned loudly but stopped short of moving his hand any lower.

"Darlin', you're killing me. I have a hotel to run and I really have to go. Oh God, I need a cold shower already."

He stood and looked down at her lying naked in his bed. Sanders couldn't believe this ravishing woman was issuing an invitation and he had to say no. He leaned over and kissed her, his lips lightly brushing hers. At that moment he wanted to kiss every inch of her body. If he didn't get out of here right now, he knew he would be lost in her again. Standing back up, he smiled the intimate smile of a lover.

"Breakfast is on the terrace," he said, his voice husky with desire. "Eat it while it's hot and enjoy the view. Then go back to sleep if you want. I'll catch up with you later and take you up on that invitation."

Sanders turned and strode purposefully from the bedroom. In a few seconds, Julie heard the outside door click shut. She stretched, got up, and put on the bathrobe she found laying across the foot of the bed. She went out to the terrace, suddenly famished, and found the table set with a tray of food, a carafe of delicious smelling coffee, and an exotic flower in a crystal vase. Her heart did a little flip at the thought that he had gone to the trouble of finding a beautiful flower for her so early in the morning.

Her stomach growled loudly so Julie began to eat heartily. She had never known that sex could create such an appetite but then she had never had sex like she had last night. As she ate her breakfast, her mind ran through last night's activities and she found that her breasts were tingling just from the thought of what Sanders did to her. Her heart was doing flip flops too and she realized she was falling in love with him. Oh boy, that was certainly

unexpected and unwanted! A relationship with
Sanders could only include amazing sex for what
remained of her vacation and then it was back to the
reality of Chicago and her medical career. Love
could not enter into this picture she told herself.

"Well," Julie said out loud. "I need to put a
shield around my heart and enjoy what he has to
offer for the next ten days. I simply cannot fall in
love with someone I barely know and I will never
see again after this vacation."

Knowing that her heart would not listen to
her mind, Julie thought some more about her
situation while she finished her breakfast. She could
avoid him and the burning sexual attraction between
them or she could enjoy the remaining days and deal
with the heartbreak when she returned to Chicago.
Not knowing exactly what she wanted to do, she sat
back and looked at his incredible ocean view. She
saw that hotel life was continuing without her. The
first snorkel lessons of the day were starting, the tiki
hut restaurant had a dozen or more breakfast
customers, and the beach side lounge chairs were
rapidly filling. She wondered how Skip was doing,
so she needed to get dressed and go find out. She
would figure out later what to do about Sanders.

While she was showering, Julie decided to
spend the day exploring the island a bit on the
bicycle she had rented. She went downstairs wearing
shorts, a tank top, sneakers, and a hat. She carried a
backpack filled with water bottles, sunscreen, and
snacks. She stopped at the front desk to pick up a
boxed lunch she had ordered from the kitchen and
find out if there was any news about Skip.

"Hi," Julie said to the receptionist. "Do you know how Skip is doing today? He pulled me out of the ocean when I passed out the other day. I'm really worried about him."

"Hi Dr. Shelton," the young lady said. "Mr. Sanders spoke to his doctor a little while ago and he's doing very well. They expect to release him in four or five days. It would be sooner if we had a doctor on the island but since we don't they want to keep him and watch for infection in his leg. They're worried because he was in the dirt by the road for about six hours before Mr. Sanders found him."

"I feel so bad for him," Julie responded. "Please let me know if I can do anything to help. I owe him my life."

"Of course," the girl replied. "By the way, Mr. Sanders said if I saw you to tell you he would be busy most of the day. He also left this note for you. Oh and here's your lunch from Miss Marie. She said to enjoy your day!"

"Thank you," Julie said as she took the envelope and the small box the girl was holding.

Opening the envelope as she walked away, Julie removed the note from Sanders.

Good morning again Darlin',
I hope you enjoyed your breakfast on the terrace.
I'm going to be very busy today since I was on the
big island most of yesterday. I talked to the doctor
and Skip is healing nicely.
Would you join me for dinner at the Birds of
Paradise restaurant for tonight's BBQ buffet?

Followed by a stroll on the beach under the stars? I hope you will. I'll look for you in the lobby at 7:00. Last night was unbelievable Julie. I don't even know where to begin in describing the most sensual, erotic experience of my life. But I guess I don't really need to since you were the reason it was what it was. I'm looking forward to tonight..... And now I need another cold shower!
Sanders

Julie smiled as she turned toward the massive wooden doors and stashed her lunch in her backpack. In that moment she decided what she wanted to do. She was going to enjoy the next ten days and deal with the aftermath when she went back to Chicago. She knew deep inside that no matter what her brain said, her heart would not rest if she didn't take this time to explore the possibilities with Sanders.

As she headed out to the bike rack, Julie was unaware that Sanders had been watching her from the hallway on the other side of the lobby. His heart did a little flip of its own when he saw her smile at his note. He knew he was feeling way too much for this bewitching stranger but he couldn't seem to resist her. When he left Texas he had decided to never again let a woman get to that place inside him where he could be hurt. And now he seemed to be rushing there without a second thought.

"I must be an idiot," he muttered to himself. "I've only known her for a few days. I can't possibly have feelings for her."

"Yeah right," he answered himself. "And in a few days when she's gone, I'm gonna be one hurt cowboy."

With that he turned and strode down the hall towards the kitchen. He needed to stay very, very busy to keep his mind occupied with something other than the enticing Dr. Shelton.

CHAPTER 8

Little Cayman was a profusion of verdant plant life and unusual wild life as Julie biked along Guy Banks Road, the narrow road that ran around the island. She had never seen such brilliant colors and lush foliage. On the west coast, she passed the dock where boats were coming in from Grand Cayman. There was a beehive of activity as tourists arrived from or departed for the big island. She saw Salt Rock Nature Trail off to the right, running deep into the forest. Further on she saw the dive boats advertising dive locations such as Sport Bay, Bloody Bay Wall, and Jackson Bay. Julie shivered as she read the roadside sign detailing the sheer drop-off in Bloody Bay where the coral reef fell into incredibly deep sea. While the descriptions of the sea creatures that can be seen were astounding, she was sure her fear of drowning would prevent her from ever seeing them.

Julie decided to stop for lunch at Bloody Bay with its magnificent mahogany forest that ran almost into the water. She could hear the Red-footed Boobies chirping a lively melody and she smiled at what a perfect day it was. She found a picnic spot on the pristine beach and enjoyed the dazzling view of clear turquoise water and bobbing dive boats while she ate Miss Marie's delicious lunch. She had wanted to continue to Grape Tree Ponds, but decided to rest on the beach instead and enjoy the island beauty all around her.

As the afternoon began to really heat up, Julie got back on the bike, consulted her map, and headed past Jackson Point to Olivine Kirk Drive. This road would take her across the island to South Hole Sound where she could pick up Guy Banks Road again and head back toward the hotel. She decided she would stop at either the Little Cayman Museum or the National Trust, home of the Booby Pond Visitor's Centre and Nature Reserve before going back to the hotel.

The road from the north shore of the island to the south shore was deserted as Julie pedaled leisurely down tree lined Olivine Kirk Drive. She was enjoying the cool breeze and shaded road when an olive green jeep suddenly came rushing towards her from the opposite direction. It was so close to her she had to swerve off the road to avoid being hit. She toppled off the bike and into the dirt, her heart beating wildly by the close call. There was something odd about the front bumper but the car was gone before her brain could register what her eyes were seeing.

Shocked and alarmed by her close encounter, Julie picked herself up and started to brush off the dirt. As she stood up, she realized the jeep had stopped. Before she could do anything, it took off with a screech of tires. She checked over her body to make sure she was uninjured. She had a few scratches on one leg but was otherwise OK. She was so rattled she decided to go directly back to the hotel.

Julie pedaled furiously now, in a hurry to reach the main road. She kept watch over her shoulder, afraid the jeep would return for a second shot at her. She breathed a sigh of relief when she could finally see South Hole Sound in front of her. She turned right and headed towards the hotel, passing the stunning waters of the Sound and then the airport without so much as a glance. She was very upset by the incident with the jeep. She had been thinking about it as she was riding and the more she thought, the more convinced she was the car was aiming for her.

"That car was trying to run me off the road!" she exclaimed out loud. "No, that's crazy. Why would someone want to run me down? I'm being paranoid because of what happened to Skip. Get a grip Dr. Shelton!"

Julie reached the hotel about four o'clock. She had three hours before her date with Sanders. As she parked the bike in the bike rack, she breathed a sigh of relief. She removed her backpack, closed her eyes, and took a deep breath. She decided she would take a long hot bath, dress, and then go to the tiki bar for a glass of wine before dinner. She turned around and smacked right into a broad chest.

"Hi Darlin', how was your day?" Sanders inquired with a smile. "You look a little flushed. Is that because you're thinking about me?"

"Oh damn!" Julie exclaimed as her backpack fell to the ground. "You startled me!"

She stepped back, picked up her backpack, and without warning, burst into tears.

"Hey, I'm sorry," Sanders said as he pulled her back against his chest. "I didn't mean to scare you sweetheart. Don't cry, please. I'm really sorry."

"No, it's not that," Julie stuttered, embarrassed that she was blubbering like a baby. "It's just that…..oh damn!"

The tears rolled down her cheeks as she put her head against his chest and snuggled into his embrace. Sanders held her tightly against him, unsure of what to do next. He hated when women cried. He always felt helpless and uneasy, like he had done something wrong. So he did the only thing he knew to do….he held her until the sobs quieted. When he thought she could speak again, Sanders stroked her hair and asked what was wrong.

"I had a close call with a car on my way back," Julie rushed to get the words out, trying to stop another onslaught of tears. "It was really scary after what happened to Skip."

The tears came anyway. Her near drowning, heat stroke, and Skip's accident coupled with her own near miss was more than she could bear. Sanders held her tighter and continued to stroke her hair. He was concerned that this strong, beautiful woman could be brought to such a tearful breakdown by a close call with a car. Something just didn't seem right to him.

"It's okay, Darlin', it's okay," he murmured to her. "Let's get you up to your room and you can tell me all about it."

They walked into the hotel lobby, Sanders arm around her shoulders. He chose the elevator as Julie seemed too fragile to take the stairs. She let them into her room and quickly collapsed on the couch. He sat softly beside her and held her as a new wave of tears rocked her body.

Finally Julie got her emotions under control and pulled away from Sanders. She excused herself and went to the bathroom to wash her face. She silently berated herself for being such a sissy and dissolving into tears in front of him. It didn't help that he was being so kind and gentle, so caring. She almost wished he would laugh at her. His tender demeanor was pushing the feelings she had for him even deeper into her heart.

When she returned to the living room, Sanders was standing looking out the sliding glass door. She watched him from behind, her heart twisting with emotion, wanting him to hold her, make love to her, take her to that spectacular high again. She caught her breath, remembering the exquisite pleasure he had given her the last two nights.

Sanders heard a noise, turned, and saw that she was standing uncertainly beside the couch. She looked ravishing, even with red eyes and dirty clothes. His heart ached for her just as much as his body wanted her. He closed the distance between them, took her hand, and led her back to the couch. He needed to understand what had caused her tears, needed to know if he was the reason she looked like a lost angel.

"What happened, Julie?" he asked, his eyes full of concern and compassion.

"I was biking on Olivine Kirk Drive towards South Hole Sound. It's so beautiful there and I guess I wasn't watching the road well. Anyway, this car came out of nowhere, going so fast, and seemed to be headed right for me. I swerved off the road and fell into the dirt and brush. The car slowed down but then sped away when I stood up."

"Oh my God!" Sanders felt his heart seize. "Are you okay? Did the car hit you?"

"I'm fine," Julie said softly. "A few scratches but luckily nothing major. It was almost surreal watching that car come towards me. I know it sounds ridiculous but it seemed like it was trying to hit me."

"After what happened to Skip, I don't think that's at all ridiculous," Sanders exclaimed. "Do you know what kind of car it was? Did you see who was driving?"

"I think it was an olive green jeep," Julie was really scared now. "I was so surprised and it happened so fast that I didn't really see much. I do have an impression of more than one person being in it."

"We need to let the police know," Sanders was pacing around the room now. "They've been watching the docks and airport for anything out of the ordinary since Skip's accident, but it's hard with so many tourists coming and going. Let me call my friend on the police force and have him take a report."

"Oh no," Julie breathed. "Do you think the person who hit and robbed Skip would still be on the island? Maybe try to hit me too?"

"I can only hope not and that this is in no way related to Skip," Sanders answered. "But I'm not taking any chances."

Sanders went to her room phone, got an outside line, and called the Little Cayman police department. Julie went to the bathroom to clean up and change clothes while he was making the call. When she returned, he was pacing the length of her small suite. She could tell he was extremely disturbed by something. She put her hand on his arm and looked into his eyes.

"Hey," she said. "Calm down, I'm fine. It's probably just an odd coincidence."

"I don't think so," Sanders replied. "We rarely have any crime on this island and now there are two hit and run accidents in just a few days. I don't believe in that kind of coincidence."

Before she could say anything further, there was a knock on the door. Sanders opened the door to a reveal short, sturdily built black man wearing a police uniform. The two men shook hands and chatted about the policeman's family for a moment.

"Dr. Julie Shelton this is Captain Howard Hall with the Little Cayman Police," Sanders said as he ushered the policeman into the room. "We have a very small police force but Captain Hall is a veteran of the Texas Rangers and one hell of a detective."

"A baseball player and a police officer?" Julie questioned. "That's a little unusual on a resume I would think."

"No, Dr. Shelton," Captain Hall laughed. "The Texas Ranger Division of the Texas Public Safety Department. I can't hit a lick with a baseball bat but I'm one hell of a good shot with a rifle."

"Oh, how embarrassing!" Julie exclaimed as she looked over to see Sanders doubled over in laughter. "I'm sorry, it's been a crazy couple of days and I'm feeling a bit disoriented right now."

"No worries," Captain Hall replied. "It can be a little confusing sometimes. Can we sit down and talk about what happened to you?"

Julie led the way into the living area and sat on the couch. Sanders sat beside her while Captain Hall sat in the wing chair next to them. Sanders took her hand, looked into her eyes, and nodded. She knew he was telling her that he was there for her.

"Dr. Shelton, please tell me what happened out there today. My department is looking into Skip Anderson's accident," the policeman said. "I need to know everything you can remember."

Julie related her story just as she had with Sanders, watching Captain Hall take careful notes. When she reached the part about the car stopping, she began to stumble a little over the words. Sanders squeezed her hand and gave her an encouraging nod. She finished her tale, took a deep breath, and looked at the Captain.

"Do you think it could be related to Skip's accident?" she asked in a quivering voice.

"I honestly don't know yet, but we will find out," Captain Hall replied. "You said the car was green. Did you notice anything else about the car? What kind it was? Make? Model? Did you see any damage or any other identifying marks?"

"Well I'm not really much into cars but when it stopped and I looked up, I had the impression it was a small jeep. The same size and color as the ones you see in the military. It had a top on it and I also had an impression there was more than one person in it. I'm sorry, but it happened so fast and I was so shocked that I didn't get a really good look."

"Don't worry, Dr. Shelton," Captain Hall said. "You had a near miss with a car and that isn't the best environment for noticing details. Let it rest in your mind for a day or so and let me know if you remember anything else. Sanders knows how to reach me if you do."

The policeman stood, as did Sanders and Julie. He shook hands with both of them and Sanders walked him to the door. The two men stood at the door and talked quietly for a few minutes before Captain Hall waved goodbye to her. Sanders returned to the room. He crossed to the sliding glass door where Julie was standing, took her in his arms and held her tightly against him.

"I'm so glad you're alright," he whispered. "I thought my heart would stop when you told me what happened."

Julie held onto him for a few minutes and then pushed away to look out at the ocean as the setting sun cast a red glow over it. She felt restless and adrift, signs she was sure were coming from the shocking events of the last few days. She had a thought that maybe she should just go back to Chicago and forget about a warm sunny vacation. But the next thought was that she didn't want to leave Sanders. It hurt deep in her heart to think of never seeing him again. She was falling in love and it scared her even more than the jeep had.

"A penny for your thoughts, Darlin'" Sanders said as he watched a parade of emotions play across her face.

73

CAYMAN KISS

He was looking at her achingly beautiful face and fighting the raging emotions dancing in his own heart. He wanted to hold her, take care of her, keep her with him for the rest of his life. He hadn't wanted to fall in love with her, but he now admitted to himself that he was very deeply in love. He didn't know how he would cope when she left to go back home to Chicago. All he knew was that he could never admit it to her and see her laugh in his face.

Julie turned and fell into his embrace. She didn't want to think, didn't want to imagine what could have happened to her, didn't want to wonder how she would be able to leave him when her vacation was over. Sanders tilted her face up with his fingers and looked into her eyes, eyes that were as blue as the ocean he loved so much. He leaned down and ever so softly kissed her. His lips were like feathers tickling her lips. The tip of his tongue flitted across her bottom lip and she parted her lips for him, sucking his tongue into the warm wet depths of her mouth. The soft, sensual kiss turned instantly passionate with a need they both felt, the need to be totally connected to each other.

Sanders groaned as her body pressed into his, her soft femininity like a flame igniting a torch inside him. He ran his hands down her arms, across her back, and then over her firm round ass. He heard her gasp as he squeezed her butt cheeks with his big hands and felt her nipples harden against his chest. She was practically panting now as she sucked his tongue even deeper into her mouth.

When he grabbed her ass, Julie felt an explosion of heat rush through her body. She knew

74

she was already wet and now she felt an overwhelming need to have his hard penis inside her. She wanted him in a way she never knew was possible. No man had ever before touched her very soul with a single kiss. No man but Sanders. She pressed herself as tightly against him as possible and felt his erection against her stomach.

"I need you, need you right now," Julie moaned. "Please baby, I want you inside me."

Sanders slowly undressed her right there in front of the window. Her skin took on the same pink glow as the evening sky when his fingers slid up her sides and pulled her tank top over her head. Her shorts came down around her hips and thighs next, his fingers tracing the length of her shapely legs down to her ankles. She was so beautiful, so perfect that he was barely able to breathe. And when he did take a breath, he smelled her arousal, her need for him. It was the most intoxicating smell in the world.

Her skin on fire from his touch, Julie began to tremble with need. Every stroke of his fingers seemed to fan the flames that were out of control inside her. She wasn't sure her legs would hold her as his fingers traced back up to her hips. Sanders reached around and unhooked her bra, freeing her breasts for his heated hands to caress. He took a gasping breath as he touched her nipples with his fingers and she gasped in return at the electric jolt that went through her body.

All that was left was her bikini panties and he wondered if they were wet from her arousal. Sliding his hands down to her hips again, Sanders reached between her legs and confirmed that the panties were

75

indeed soaked, causing Julie to gasp once again as his fingers lightly touched her through the fabric. He pushed the panties past her hips and let them fall to the floor. She was totally naked now and he wanted her with such a force that it shook him to his core. He had never wanted a woman the way he wanted this one. His world was reduced to giving her pleasure in every way possible, bringing to orgasm over and over. He wanted her to be focused on nothing but the incredible sensations pulsing through her body.

"Oh God please," Julie moaned. "I need you inside me baby, I need to come so bad."

Sanders thought he might explode at that moment. She wanted him as much as he wanted her. He knew the minute he was inside her, all control would be gone. He couldn't take her just yet, he wanted to extend her pleasure for as long as possible. Still fully clothed, Sanders sat Julie on the edge of the bed and told her to lay back with her legs up in the air. He knelt on the floor and slid his hands down the insides of her thighs, pushing her legs open in the process. He slowly caressed her inner thighs up and down, up and down. She was moaning non-stop now and beginning to thrash about, begging for release.

He leaned forward and licked her belly button, careful not to touch that sensitive area below. Sanders was teasing her now with his tongue, licking down to her pubic hair but stopping short of her heat and wetness. He continued to caress and lick her hot skin, turning it from pink to red where his hands and tongue touched. She was arching up, trying to rub

76

her pussy against him but he wasn't ready for that yet. Instead he trailed his fingers down her long legs once again, licked the back of her knees, and then blew hot breath onto her swollen clitoris.

"Ooooooh," Julie whimpered as her body tensed, wanting to come. "Oooooohhhhhhhh!!!"

Sanders continued to lick and caress her everywhere except the one place she wanted the most. After what seemed an eternity to Julie, he leaned forward and licked her pussy lips and then her clit in a single long stroke of his tongue. She screamed as a huge orgasm rocked her and then begged for his hard penis to be inside her. But the begging suddenly stopped as his tongue began a feverish assault on her. She came again and again and again, each orgasm even more mind blowing than the last.

The next hour became a non-stop orgasm for Julie. Each time she thought she could take no more, Sanders would lick and suck her to another inconceivable level with his tongue and fingers. Her world was nothing more than the astonishing pleasure suffusing her entire body. Her orgasms became an experience that penetrated every pore of her being and she was overwhelmed by sensations that she had not known were possible.

Finally he stopped and stood to look at her. Sanders face was wet with her juices and his eyes were black as coal. He had never been so aroused, never needed someone as badly as he did now. His huge erection was bulging in his pants and his brain was demanding that he do something about it. He quickly stripped his clothes off and climbed onto the bed. He pulled Julie over to him and held her while she tried to calm her breathing. His hands continued to caress her arms, her back, and her butt. He was in agony with need but wanted her to be ready for him, wanted her to be ready for another massive orgasm.

Julie's hand began to glide over his chest as her lips grazed against his shoulder. Her only thought was that she still wanted him, needed him, had to have him inside her. She didn't analyze how that could be after the last hour. She could only act on it, so she took his hard penis in her hand and slowly, slowly, slowly stroked it. Sanders groaned as her fingers clasped his hardness. When she leaned over and licked the tip of his penis he thought he would die from the electric shock that went through him.

Realizing that he was fighting for control, Julie rolled on top of his legs and licked him again. She eased her body up the length of his, her tongue sliding over his stomach as her breasts enveloped his penis. She stroked him with her breasts for a few minutes but it was more than she could take. She needed him inside her. She moved up farther until she was straddling him, his hard penis barely an inch from her dripping wet pussy.

Sanders could feel the heat coming from her and knew he had to be inside her right now. He grabbed her hips and positioned her pussy directly over his erect penis. He slowly lowered her onto him, her heat and wetness surrounding his pulsing shaft, her moans filling his ears. When he was totally inside, he made one small thrust with his hips. Julie screamed as the orgasm exploded in her. She threw her head back and clenched his hardness with her convulsing pussy. He grabbed her breasts with his hands and pinched her nipples as she continued to moan and come.

His own orgasm mere seconds away, Sanders moved his hands to Julie's hips and pulled her tightly against him. He began to thrust up inside her, his hands keeping her from moving. The motion of his penis stroking inside her and his pubic bone grinding against her clit sent Julie over the edge. She was again coming non-stop as he pushed deeper and deeper into her. With one final, deep push, he shouted her name and erupted with the most incredible, intense orgasm of his life.

CHAPTER 9

They awoke to a dark sky, arms and legs tangled together, Julie still on top of Sanders. She rolled off and looked up at the ceiling trying not to think about her growing feelings for him. She had almost succeeded when he spoke.

"I'm so glad you didn't get hurt today. After what those bastards did to Skip, it would have been more than I could bear if you had been injured too."

Julie's heart soared when she heard the caring and tenderness in his voice. Was it possible he had feelings for her too? She wanted to say something but had no idea how to approach the subject. Her minimal experience with men was certainly showing. Before she could think of the right thing to say he spoke again.

"Howie thinks they're holed up in the woods somewhere. The entire police force consists of six men so he doesn't have a lot of extra men to mount a search. He said something about getting additional support from Grand Cayman's force to search the island. The sooner the better as far as I'm concerned. I don't like having this kind of thing happening on my island. "

"So Captain Hall thinks it's the same car that ran down both Alex and me?" Julie asked in a shaky voice.

"This hasn't been made public but he's had several reports of a jeep-like vehicle traveling at a high rate of speed on the main road at night," Sanders related. "Each of these was followed the next day by a report of a robbery, usually tourists. After Alex was hit, he put civilian patrols at several points around the island during the night hours to supplement his meager police presence. These people must have realized it and now they've gotten bold and are out in broad daylight."

Julie shivered and Sanders pulled her close, wrapping his big arms around her. She felt safe and secure in his massive embrace. She was so in love at that moment she thought her heart would burst. She wished she could tell him, but the possibility of rejection was something she wasn't ready to deal with right now. She remained silent and snuggled deeper into his arms.

"Are you okay?" he asked. "You seem a little restless."

"It must be because I'm hungry," she stammered. "We probably missed the buffet you wanted to go to."

"Well now Darlin', that clock on the nightstand says it's ten o'clock. We sure did miss the buffet," Sanders replied. "However, I happen to know a kitchen we can raid and fix something to eat. We just have to clean up afterwards or Miss Marie will be serving my head on a platter for lunch tomorrow."

They made their way to the hotel's kitchen and fixed a quick supper of fruit, cheese, wine and homemade bread. As they sat at a small table to one side of the kitchen, Sanders asked Julie what her plans were for the following day.

"I had planned to go to the Nature Reserve and the museum today so maybe I'll do that tomorrow," she replied. "This is such a beautiful island that I don't want to miss any of the sights. I loved the beach at Bloody Bay with those amazing mahogany trees running right up to the sand. I could sit on that beach forever I think."

The thought ran through Sanders' head that he wished he could sit next to her on a beach forever. This fascinating woman was turning him inside out. He knew she would be leaving soon but he couldn't stop himself from wanting to be with her while she was here.

"How about hanging around the hotel at the beach or pool in the morning," he heard himself say. "I can get away in the afternoon and I'll take you to a beach that will make Bloody Bay look shabby."

"Where?" Julie asked, thrilled that he wanted to spend the afternoon with her.

"Let's make it a surprise," he responded. "I'll get Miss Marie to pack a lunch and we can leave about one o'clock."

"If you're sure you can take the time off, I'd love that," she said.

"It's set then," Sanders exclaimed, his heart soaring at the thought of spending the entire afternoon and evening with her. "Now let's clean this up so I don't end up on Miss Marie's bad side."

They quickly cleaned the kitchen and headed down the hall towards the main reception area. As they waited at the elevator, Julie turned to look at him. She wanted to invite him to her room for the night but suddenly felt shy and unsure. Damn, she wished she had more experience with this kind of thing. She could stitch a gash on a child's forehead

with a steady hand or convince an eighty year-old
man that he did indeed need to take his blood
pressure meds. When she found herself standing face
to face with this man, she was shaking and tongue-
tied.

Sanders saw Julie's face pale slightly when
she turned towards him. She clasped her hands
together and he could see they were shaking. He
thought she was having a delayed reaction to her
afternoon experience. He pushed the button for the
elevator and spoke.

"How about I go up with you? You look a
little pale and it worries me."

"Yeah, that's probably a good idea," Julie
said, relieved that she didn't have to ask him to her
room.

The elevator arrived and they went upstairs.
Once they were inside her room, Julie was again
nervous. She felt a growing need to kiss him, touch
him, feel him against her skin but she wasn't sure
how to tell him. Yes, she had been a bit bold the
other night but tonight she felt unsure.

Watching her pace around the room sending
glances his way, Sanders suddenly realized that she
was nervous about him. He wanted her to be totally
at ease and enjoy the days they had left. When her
pacing brought her near, he reached out and grabbed
her arm. She folded herself into his arms and looked
up at him. He looked into her eyes and ran his hand
the length of her beautiful blonde hair. When he
spoke, his voice was heavy with desire.

"You're the most sensual, electrifying
woman I've ever known. Watching you for the last

few minutes made me crazy with need. I need you Darlin', need you right now."

Sanders lowered his head and brushed her lips with his. That simple touch set him on fire, body and soul. He was consumed with a need he had never felt before, a need that only Julie could fill. The kiss deepened as he pressed his lips harder against hers and her mouth opened to accept his tongue. They stood in the middle of the room, bodies pressed so tightly together they could feel each other's heart beat. Her mouth tasted of wine and was as hot and wet as her pussy had been earlier in the evening. He groaned as his penis became fully erect at the thought of sliding into her heated body.

Julie's own need for Sanders was so strong she was sure she would die if he didn't take her soon. She wanted him inside her at that very moment and wanted to keep him inside her forever. She needed him so badly she was dizzy with desire. With his arms still around her, she grabbed the hem of his shirt and pushed it up over his head. Her tongue found his chest and licked a hot trail from his lips down to his neck and then down to his nipples. She licked and nipped them, marveling at how small and hard they were. Never before had she found a man's nipples so arousing.

Without warning, Sanders picked her up and took her to the bed. He put her on her feet next to the bed and began undressing her. When she stood naked before him he sucked in a deep breath, amazed at the perfection of her body. He knew it was made for him, just him, and he wanted to know every single inch of it. He quickly removed his

84

CAYMAN KISS

sandals and pants, his penis erect and pulsing when
freed.

Julie looked down at his erection, awed that a
kiss could render this reaction. She was acutely
aware that he obviously wanted her very, very
much….as much as she wanted him. She was wet
and hot, needing him as much as he needed her. She
looked up into his eyes and saw that they were again
black with desire. She could see into his soul and
could feel him looking into hers. She had never
known such a connection before.

Sanders took her by the hand and they lay
down on the bed. He kissed her again as his hands
explored her breasts and belly. When his fingers
slipped between her legs, Julie immediately arched
up and had an orgasm that suffused her entire body.
Just as quickly, his fingers, now slick with her
wetness, moved on down her thighs, over her knees,
and across her shins.

"Roll over Darlin'," Sanders whispered in a
voice thick with yearning. "Let me see that perfect
ass."

Julie rolled onto her stomach, her pussy still
quivering from coming. She could feel wetness
running down her thighs and knew she was only
minutes from another incredible orgasm. Sanders
straddled her butt and began to lick the back of her
neck. She could feel his hardness pushing against
her and moaned. His tongue moved to her shoulders
and then moved lower, leaving a hot, wet trail down
her spine. Grabbing the sheets with both hands, Julie
moaned even louder as his tongue pushed her to the
edge.

CAYMAN KISS

When he reached her butt, Sanders sighed.
He was in heaven, his lips kissing her firm, round
ass, his tongue flicking out to taste her skin. He
spent what felt like hours simply licking, kissing,
and caressing her ass. She moaned when he put even
the slightest pressure on her butt cheeks and he
realized he was pressing her clit against the bed
occasionally. He could smell the scent of her arousal
and it inflamed him even more. He wanted this
beautiful, sensual woman in the worst way. He
moved lower and spread her legs with his. His hard
penis brushed against her butt crack and he swore
under his breath as he tried to maintain control. He
wasn't finished with her yet, wasn't ready to grant
himself the release he so desperately wanted.

Kneeling between her spread legs, Sanders
leaned over and licked the small of her back. His
tongue flicked out and made a trail down her butt
crack toward her heated pussy. He pushed her legs
farther apart and flicked his tongue against her pussy
lips. He licked her wetness and plunged his tongue
into her, his big hands pushing her pelvis against the
bed.

Julie screamed as she came the first time, her
hands pulling the sheets loose as she strained
upward. The second and third orgasms were just as
intense as the first, Sanders' tongue and hands
relentless in their mission to bring her pleasure.
After the fourth or fifth, he reached the point where
he could no longer live if he wasn't inside her. He
wanted to be in her and see that magnificent ass
while he was stroking her.

"Get up on your knees, Darlin'," he croaked as he moved back slightly. "Let me see you from behind."

Julie got on her knees and spread her legs. She had only one focus....she wanted him inside her, stroking her, taking her to that next level. Sanders moved between her legs and rubbed the tip of his penis down her butt crack. She moaned as that simple act sent a jolt of electricity through her entire body. When he touched the head against her pussy lips, she cried out, begging him to put it inside her, to make her come.

Hearing her pleas sent Sanders over the edge. He could no longer control himself, he had to have her now. With a single, hard thrust he was inside her, her heat and wetness surrounding his hard, throbbing penis, her beautiful ass soft as silk under his fingers. He groaned in pleasure and heard her whimper "Oh God". He was totally gone now and began thrusting in and out of her with abandon. He was aware of her cries and felt her pussy gripping his penis as she came over and over again.

"Oooooooohhhh, oooooooohhhhhh Sanders!!" she shouted as she came once more.

That was all he could take. He grabbed her hips and pulled her back to him. His rock hard penis pushed deep into her and he shouted her name as he had the most astounding orgasm of his life. His hot juices filled her as she screamed his name one more time. And then there was quiet as they fell to the mattress, struggling for breath.....both spent and exhausted by the intensity of their love making.

CAYMAN KISS

CHAPTER 10
THE KISS

The next afternoon, Sanders was true to his promise of the evening before. He and Julie took a picnic lunch packed by Miss Marie and biked over to South Hole Sound. From there they kayaked to tiny Owens Island, a spot of land with the most beautiful beach Julie had ever seen. When they first reached the island, she stepped out of the kayak, stood in the water and gaped at the unspoiled sandy beach that ringed the island. The white sand sparkled in the brilliant sunlight and the water lapping the shore was an amazing clear blue that defied words.

"Cat got your tongue, Darlin'?" Sanders teased as he watched her jaw drop and her eyes open wide.

"It's so fabulous I don't even know what to say!" Julie gushed. "I've never seen anything like this."

"We aim to please ma'am," Sanders drawled as he pulled the kayak up on the sand. "This is without a doubt my most favorite spot in the world."

"I can certainly see why," Julie replied. "I feel like we're a million miles away from anyone even though I can see Little Cayman just across the sound."

"Wait until we get to the other side of the island," Sanders said. "The closest thing to that side is Cayman Brac but it's five miles away. We'll be totally alone."

"What are we waiting for? Let's go!"

89

Julie was running up the beach now, motioning to Sanders to follow her. She was having a wonderful time and couldn't wait to see the other side of the island.

"Hold your horses pretty lady," Sanders laughed. "I believe we have a few things to take with us and I'm not gonna carry everything!"

"But that's why I brought you along," Julie giggled. "My own personal cabana boy to paddle the kayak and carry all my belongings."

"Cabana boy? Cabana *boy*? I'll show you what this cabana *boy* is all about young lady!"

Sanders laughed again, dropped the backpack he was holding, and ran after her. He reached her in four long strides and pulled her to him. His kiss this time was anything but gentle. His lips ground against hers as his tongue entered her mouth. His hands grabbed her ass and she was pressed against his crotch before she knew what happened. She felt his erection and moaned.

Unable to wriggle free, Julie melted into him, heat rising in her body like a supercharged flame. Without warning Sanders broke the embrace and let go of her, laughing as she tumbled backward onto the sand. She looked up indignantly then suddenly burst into another fit of giggles.

"I get it, I get it," she tittered. "You are definitely not a boy! So what can I carry?"

"Just in case you still have any doubts, I'll be glad to make it very clear once we get to the other side of the island," he grinned lecherously at her. "But I need nourishment first. Why don't we eat up there by the tree line before we explore. One less thing to carry with us."

Julie agreed and they spread a blanket in a shady spot where the beach met the forest. Miss Marie's lunch of lobster salad with avocados and fresh pineapple bread was delicious. After carefully packing up all their trash and putting it in the kayak, they were ready to explore the rest of the island. The walk up the beach was stunning with soft, white sand underfoot and lush foliage coming almost to the water line is some places. There wasn't another soul anywhere to be seen.

The other side of the island was a short walk and when they reached it, Julie was once again speechless. There was nothing to be seen but miles and miles of clear blue water gently lapping at the sparkling white sand beach. It was like they had been dropped onto a deserted island and were the only people inhabiting this side of the world. When she finally found her voice, it was low and reverent.

"Where have I been for the last thirty years that I didn't know something like this existed?" she whispered as she dropped her backpack to the ground. "I could stay here forever."

Sanders came up behind Julie and encircled her waist with his arms. He put his mouth near her ear and whispered too, afraid to break the spell this magnificent beach had put on her.

"The first time I saw it I felt the same way," he said softly. "Now four years later, I don't know how I could live without it. I come over here often to sit and think. It's like the aura of this place has the ability to heal. It definitely healed me."

They stood silently for several minutes taking in the natural beauty of this spot. Then Julie turned and looked at him. Once again she saw the sadness in his eyes. She was about to ask him why he needed to be healed when he stepped back and dropped his backpack to the sand.

"Last one in the water has to carry both backpacks when we go back for the kayak!" he shouted as he stripped off his shirt and ran toward the water.

"Oh so not fair!" she shouted in return as she stripped down to her bikini and ran to the water after him.

They spent the next hour splashing, floating, and enjoying the warm Caribbean waters. When they came back up on the beach, they spread a blanket out in the shade at the edge of the forest. Water bottles appeared from the backpacks and they lounged on the blanket enjoying the peace and beauty that surrounded them. Julie was the first to break the silence.

"This is definitely a place of healing, Sanders," she said quietly. "I haven't felt this good, this at peace with myself in many months. I feel like I'm finally ready to go on with my life. Thank you for sharing this special place with me."

"It's what kept me sane in the first few months after I moved here," he replied. "You're the only person I've shared this with."

"What happened that you left Texas and ended up here?" Julie turned to look at him. "I don't mean to pry but sometimes I see such sadness in your eyes."

"It's a long story," Sanders sighed and turned back to look at the water. "But the short version....well my wife, the only woman I ever loved, left me for my business partner. Later I found out they had been having an affair for several years. I sold my half of the business and left Texas. I thought I could leave all the hurt behind. But I found that the hurt was still there, tearing me up every day. I threw myself into building my hotel and when things felt overwhelming, I came here. Slowly, slowly, slowly the hurt has faded away."

He turned to look at her and was surprised to see tears sliding down her face. He wiped them away with his thumb and brushed her lips with his.

"It's okay Darlin'," he whispered. "Don't feel sorry for me. I'll probably never marry again but I'll be fine."

"I don't feel sorry for you," Julie stuttered. "I mean, I do feel sorry.....but I don't....oh damn!"

She dissolved into tears again and Sanders was at a loss as to what to do. This was certainly not the reaction he had expected from her. What happened in Texas was sad, but he wasn't the only man, or woman for that matter, who had been cheated on. Then it dawned on him.....she wasn't crying about what had happened to him. This had to be far more personal to reduce her to this kind of sobbing. Something horrible had happened to her, something even worse than the events of the last few days.

"Tell me Darlin', tell me what happened," he crooned as he folded her in his arms.

"I don't know if I can talk about it," Julie sobbed. "It hurt so much I thought I would die."

"You can talk to me," Sanders said softly, his lips brushing her hair. "Whatever it is, you're strong and you'll survive. And I'll listen whenever you're ready to tell me."

Julie struggled to get her breath and then began to talk. She told Sanders about Michael, about their dating while she was doing her residency, about how they had planned a February wedding, and finally about how he had dumped her on Thanksgiving Day after dinner with her family.

"He told me he was in love with one of the lawyers he worked with," she said, tears streaming from her eyes. "He said it was my fault, that I never had time for him. He said I'm in love with my job and my patients and there wasn't enough of me left for him. We were supposed to be in the Swiss Alps right now on our honeymoon."

Sanders' heart was breaking for this sweet, smart, amazing woman. How could that idiot man make her think his cheating was all her fault? What an asshole!

"Sweetheart you need to understand one basic thing," he replied as he held her tighter. "A cheat is a cheat and it has nothing to do with the person they are with. He made the choice to cheat on you and it would have happened whether you were a doctor or a housewife. It took me a long time to realize that."

"What made you realize it?" Julie asked in a shaky voice. "I so want to believe that it wasn't my fault but I know that my job took up a lot of my time and energy. I thought he didn't mind because he worked long hours too."

"I finally realized that it wasn't about me at all when I heard that my ex-wife is getting divorced again," Sanders replied with an edge in his voice. "Apparently she has a new man in her life. My former business partner is devastated and called to commiserate about what a bitch she is. I hung up on him."

"Oh," Julie remarked quietly and her heart went out to him.

"Did you ever think that maybe the long hours your ex spent at work was a cover for his cheating?" he continued, furious with a man he had never even heard of until ten minutes ago. "Cheaters don't ever want to take the blame for their actions. They try hard to get the other person to shoulder all the blame."

"I thought about it once or twice but it's almost as hard to think that you could so seriously underestimate someone," she answered. "How can I trust my instincts with people when I couldn't even see that someone I trusted with my life and my heart was involved with another woman?"

"I know Darlin'," Sanders responded. "I know exactly how you feel. I also know that one day you will accept that we all make mistakes when the heart is involved."

They sat silently for a short while, Julie wrapped in Sanders arms, both of them lost in their thoughts. As she looked at the water, Julie began to feel stronger inside. Her heart still hurt over Michael's betrayal but not nearly as bad as it had when she arrived on Little Cayman. Maybe this little spit of land did have healing powers.

Sanders' thoughts were going in an entirely different direction. He knew he was deeply in love with Julie and was headed for another major heartache in a few short days. He had survived one and he hoped he would survive this one too. She would return to Chicago, go back to work, and smile when she thought of her little fling in the Caymans. He would feel the pain again and was sure he would be spending a lot more time on Owens Island.

Julie turned to look at Sanders, her eyes smoldering with passion. She wanted to start her new life right this minute and this man would help her. She knew their time was short and he certainly didn't feel in his heart what she felt. But she wanted to try to obliterate the hurt and betrayal and knew this handsome, complicated, bewildering man was exactly what the doctor ordered. She would mourn his loss when she returned to Chicago, but at this moment the only thing she wanted was to make love to him.

She kissed him softly on the lips and stroked his bare chest with her hand. A quiet sigh escaped her lips. Being with him felt so right….nothing had ever felt this right before. He returned the kiss, softly at first then with a growing intensity as her hands caressed his arms and shoulders. His hands moved across her shoulders to her back and his rough palms slid down her spine. The tingling in her lower body soon became a flame that filled her entire being. She briefly wondered how a kiss and a simple caress could ignite a passion that totally consumed her, body and soul.

Unknown to Julie, Sanders was thinking the same thing. Her soft kiss and her silky hands had aroused him to unbelievable desire in mere minutes. He had never wanted a woman the way he wanted this one. He had never felt so connected to a woman as he did to this one. He knew in that moment there would never be another woman in his life who completed him the way Julie did.

The kiss deepened as their tongues met and their hands moved slowly over each other's bodies. Without breaking contact with her lips, Sanders untied Julie's bikini top and took a perfect breast in each hand. He gently squeezed them and ran his thumb over her hard nipples. His lips quivered against hers as she drew in a long breath and shivered with need. He understood….his need was just as great as hers.

He laid her back on the blanket and slipped her bikini bottom down over her hips, past her knees, pulling them over her feet. He kissed her stomach, her thighs, her knees, and finally her feet as he pulled the tiny scrap of cloth down. He looked up from her feet and his eyes feasted on her body, so lush and ripe, so soft and inviting. When his eyes reached her lips, he felt drawn to kiss them again, to continue the slow sensuous dance of their tongues. It was so simple……his lips had to be against hers.

He stood and quickly pushed his swim trunks down, stepping out of them when they hit the blanket. Julie looked up, first at his huge erection and then into his eyes. Sanders knew without words that she wanted him inside her, needed him as much as he needed her. He knelt between her legs, leaned over, and kissed her pussy lips and clit, wanting her to be ready for him. She moaned and arched up, spreading her legs wider in invitation. He saw glistening beads of moisture and thought he would explode right then knowing this astonishing woman was so wet and ready from a kiss.

Sanders moved up until his lips were on her stomach, between her breasts, and then on her neck. No tongue, no hands, nothing but whispery kisses setting her skin on fire. When his lips met hers again, they both moaned as the heat seemed to seal their lips together. They continued the kiss that had aroused both of them to such heights….tongues doing a slow dance first in her mouth, then in his.

On top of her now, Sanders rubbed his chest against her nipples while his tongue licked slowly across her lips. He felt her moan against his lips when his rock hard penis touched her hard little clit. He entered her then, very, very slowly, sliding his tongue into her mouth as he slid his penis into the center of her heat.

When Sanders entire length was sheathed by Julie's wetness, he stopped moving. His skin was on fire where it touched hers. He kissed her nose, her chin, her neck….the feel of her skin against his lips driving him to madness. He returned to her lips, his tongue again sliding into her mouth as his hips began to move of their own accord. He stroked her in long slow movements with his penis and his tongue. He wanted to stay like this, his tongue in her mouth, his hard penis inside her, making love to her forever.

CAYMAN KISS

When he entered her, Julie lost the ability to think of anything but Sanders' mouth and throbbing penis. Her world focused solely on the feel of his tongue in her mouth and his penis sliding deep into her pussy. When she thought she could take no more and would explode from the incredible sensations, she felt him break the kiss.

Now his lips languidly caressed her nose, her chin, her neck. The heat seared her flesh. His skin pressing against her skin became an inferno raging through her entire body. His lips returned to hers and she felt his tongue slide back into her mouth. When his hips began to move, slowly thrusting his penis in and out of her, she felt an unbelievable orgasm building inside her. She wanted to stay like this, his tongue in her mouth, his hard penis inside her, making love to him forever.

His slow thrusts continued pushing her higher and higher until the orgasmic wave was huge and roaring in her ears. Julie came, screaming his name against his lips as they rode to heights neither had known possible. Over and over, one orgasm blended into the next, engulfing her entire body. Fighting to control his own orgasm, Sanders was awed feeling her moan and scream from the slow movement of his tongue and penis. She sucked his tongue with each thrust of his penis, taking both deeper in to the heat of her body.

It was finally too much for his sensory overloaded brain and Sanders gave in, unable to wait a single second longer to join Julie on that crashing wave. He thrust deep into her and, murmuring her name against her lips, came with a ferocity that shook him to his core. She came too, as if her body knew it was time to push them both over the edge.

He lay on top of her, their lips still touching, unable to move for several minutes afterward. He kissed her deeply once more, looked into her eyes, and whispered her name. Julie saw so much emotion in his eyes that her breath caught in her chest. Could it be that he had feelings for her too? She was too far gone to think straight and the thought flitted away. Sanders reluctantly broke the kiss and rolled off her. He put an arm around her and pulled her against him until her head was on his shoulder. Neither spoke for a long time….words were simply not necessary.

When the wave finally subsided, Sanders shifted slightly and turned to look at Julie. He smiled and ran a finger over her lips. He was still amazed that a kiss could be so erotic and sensual, could take them both to such heights of sexual pleasure.

"As much as I would like to stay here for hours tasting your lips, we need to start back. The sun will be down in an hour or so and we need to be back on Little Cayman by then. A kayak on the ocean isn't the best place to be after dark."

Julie ran her finger over his lips, equally in awe of where that kiss had taken both of them. She kissed him lightly and sat up. She could see the sun was getting low in the horizon. With her fear of drowning, she certainly didn't want to be bobbing around in the ocean after dark. They gathered their things, dressed, and headed down the beach to the other side of the island. When they reached the kayak and stowed everything inside, she turned to him.

"Thank you for sharing this place with me. It's so beautiful and it definitely has the power to heal. This is the best afternoon I've had in a very long time," she said as she again touched his lips with her finger. "I'll treasure this memory for the rest of my life."

CHAPTER 11

It was a beautiful ride back to Little Cayman. Julie and Sanders watched the sun sinking towards the water as the kayak slid quietly over the clear blue water. When they arrived at the Sunset Inn, the hotel lobby was bubbling with excitement.

"Mr. Sanders!" Lisa, the evening receptionist, shouted as they walked in the door. "Skip is here!! We have him settled in Room 328 like you said and everyone is taking turns sitting with him when they're not on shift."

"Skip is here?" Julie asked. "I thought he had to stay in the hospital for a few days."

"Well Darlin'," Sanders drawled. "They were keeping him to watch for infection. I asked if he could be released to me. I told them he could stay at the hotel while he recovered and that we had a top notch doctor staying here who would be happy to check his wounds everyday. I hope you don't mind."

"Not at all!" Julie exclaimed. "It's the least I can do after he saved my life. But why didn't you tell me?"

"When we left this afternoon, I wasn't sure if they were going to let him go," Sanders replied. "Looks like they decided it would be okay."

They walked across the lobby to the front desk. Lisa and several other hotel employees were crowded around chattering about the afternoon's excitement.

"The helicopter was so awesome!" Lisa cried. "It was like we had royalty landing on the beach!! Mr. Sanders, that was really a cool thing for you to do."

"Helicopter?" Julie inquired with a raised eyebrow.

"I had a helicopter on standby so Skip could be transported easily if they released him," Sanders answered. "No big deal."

He turned to the front desk and scanned the employees standing there.

"I know everyone's excited about Skip but we do have a hotel full of guests that need your attention," he said in his best boss' voice. "How about you take care of them while Dr. Shelton and I check up on Skip?"

Julie looked at him, ready to ask about the helicopter again, when Sanders took her by the hand and dragged her to the elevator.

"Let's go check on your patient, please. I'll take all questions later."

Julie laughed and entered the elevator, glad to be able to help the young man who had pulled her from the water. She was so happy that Skip was going to be all right. She was curious too about this man who was so loyal to his employees that he would have a helicopter on standby! Oh yes, she had questions for sure.

They reached Skip's room and found five people watching over him. Everyone was talking at once, thrilled to have him back and curious about his injuries. Julie took one look at Skip's face and decided her patient needed sleep more than anything right now.

"Sorry folks, but I think Skip needs to get some rest. I'm sure the helicopter ride wore him out and he's ready for a nap. Plus I need a little privacy while I check him over," she said with a smile. "You can come back in a few hours when he's more rested."

The group wished Skip well as Sanders shooed them out the door. Julie went into doctor mode and did a quick but thorough examination. She was very impressed with the care he had received in the Grand Cayman hospital. His leg had been broken pretty badly but had started healing. He had several bad gashes on his arms and legs that had been stitched up. The skin that was not gashed was covered in abrasions where he had obviously slid on the asphalt.

"How are you feeling?" Julie asked as she checked the bandages covering the stitches. "I can see you had excellent care at the hospital."

"I'm really tired. Thanks for sending everyone out," Skip replied. "I know they mean well but all I want to do is sleep."

"That's perfectly normal," Julie said. "Your body is trying hard to heal your fractured leg and fight infection. It's using up your energy in the process. For the next few days, you need to rest a lot. Don't be afraid to tell your well-meaning co-workers to leave when you need to sleep. If that doesn't work, call me and I'll be the bad guy."

"Thanks Dr. Shelton," Skip answered with a grin. "If they won't go, I'll give you a call."

"Not a problem Skip. Bad guy is part of the job description. The bandages look good but will need to be changed tonight. I'll stop by before I go to bed. Be sure to drink plenty of fluids and take advantage of Miss Marie's meals. If you need anything, I'm just down the hall in Room 304."

"Skip, if you can't reach Dr. Shelton or need anything at all, call the reception desk," Sanders added. "They always know where I am and I'll find Dr. Shelton for you. I'll have a dinner tray sent up right away."

"Why don't you take a nap first?" Julie cut in. "I think that's more important right now than food. I'm sure the helicopter ride was exciting and tiring, plus you had all those people wandering around in here."

"I defer to the doctor," Sanders said with a grin and a small bow.

"Sorry Mr. Sanders, but I think Dr. Shelton is the boss right now," Skip chuckled. "And I intend to listen to every word the beautiful doctor says. She sure doesn't look like any doctor I ever had before!"

"Yeah, if she walked in the exam room I'd be too flustered to remember why I was at the doctor's office," Sanders laughed.

"That's enough you guys. I'm at a severe disadvantage right now. My patients in Chicago have never seen me in a bikini," Julie replied as she pointed to the door. "So why don't we let Skip rest while I shower and put on some doctor-like clothes? Sanders, out. Go! Now!"

"I'm going, I'm going," Sanders grinned as he headed toward the door. "Skip call the desk when you wake up and tell whoever is on that you're ready to eat. I'll be sure they have a keycard to get in. From the look of things, I don't think you will have any problems with loneliness. If anything, we might need a traffic cop in the hallway!"

"Thanks Mr. Sanders," Skip answered in a serious tone. "You have no idea how much I appreciate all of this. When I was in that ditch unable to move, I was sure I would die out there. I owe you my life. You have my loyalty forever."

"You're welcome Skip. Now get some rest before the pretty lady doctor gets all riled up at both of us," Sanders said.

"Skip, I'll be around later this evening to check on you," Julie responded. She picked up a folder full of documents and scanned over them.

"The doctor's notes from Grand Cayman say not to put any weight on that leg yet, so stay in bed please. It looks like you have everything you need at hand, but if not, call the front desk. No walking around for any reason! I'll see you later and we'll get your bandages changed and meds situated."

They went out the door, leaving Skip to sleep. They walked toward Julie's room in silence. When they reached the door, Julie turned to Sanders and smiled.

"What you did for him was amazing," she exclaimed. "Not many employers would charter a helicopter and give up a hotel room for an injured employee."

"When I came here I was totally alone. I built my little hotel and hand picked my staff. My staff has become my family, Julie," he revealed. "I take care of them the best I can and they do their best for me. It's the way I ran my business in Texas and the way I run my business here. These people mean a lot to me."

"Alex told me at breakfast the other morning that you're building a medical clinic," Julie suddenly remembered.

"The people of Little Cayman adopted me and watch out for me," Sanders added. "They're my extended family. It's ridiculous that they have to go to Grand Cayman for medical care, so I decided to do something about it."

"That's quite an investment," Julie noted.

"Darlin', I have more money than I could ever spend in my lifetime. I have no family except for some distant cousins. The people on this little island are real and they're good to me and if I can help them by spending some of my money, then I'm going to do it," he said in a quiet voice.

"Don't get me wrong," she responded, looking into his eyes. "I think it's great that you're making life better for them. I guess I didn't understand your connection to the people on the island. And I didn't realize you had no family. That's something we have in common, Sanders. I have some distant relatives but my immediate family is gone too. That's why I throw myself into my work and get caught up in my patient's lives. Sometimes I wonder if Michael was jealous of them and that's why he was so upset about how much time I spent at work. But it really doesn't matter anymore. I have no one but my patients now. They managed to keep me together through the breakup and I'll be there for them no matter what."

She looked so sad and so lost that Sanders thought his heart would break. He pulled her against his chest, kissed the top of her head, and held her tight. His mind began to spin with possibilities. Could he ask Julie to move to the island and be the doctor at his new medical clinic? Could they have something more than a short fling? Would she even consider such a drastic move? Just as quickly the negative thoughts pushed in. She had a life in Chicago. She hadn't said anything about having feelings for him. Why would she want to give up what she had for him and for people she didn't even know?

Julie's mind was racing too. She wondered if Sanders had a doctor lined up for the medical clinic. She would love the job and love being with him. How could she ask about the clinic doctor without appearing too eager, too interested? But why would she want to move here? He hadn't expressed any feelings for her beyond their sexual connection. How could she even think about being here if being with him wasn't part of the equation? At least in Chicago the chances of running into Michael were very slim. If she was living on this tiny island and working in his clinic, there would be no way to avoid Sanders. Seeing him with someone else would kill her soul. She sighed into his massive chest, knowing she couldn't bring the subject up, couldn't stand the rejection she was sure she would experience.

They finally separated and Sanders looked at her. God, he was falling in love with this enchanting woman, but he couldn't tell her so. She had a life somewhere else and was recovering from a bad experience. He was simply her "rebound guy" and when her two weeks here were over, she would go home to her medical practice and her patients. Eventually she would fall in love with someone who, in return, would love her the way she deserved to be loved. He would be a brief memory she smiled about sometimes when her husband wasn't around.

"Well Darlin'," he said. "I need to check to see what else happened while we were enjoying our afternoon. How about we get together for dinner later? Maybe seven-thirty?

"Sounds good," Julie replied, glad he had interrupted her thoughts. "I need a shower and a little quiet time. Should I meet you in the lobby?"

"Yes ma'am," Sanders said. "I'm going to see if Miss Marie can rustle up something for us to have later. I think I'm too tired to try and go anywhere else tonight. Do you mind eating in my apartment tonight?"

"Since it's the most exclusive dining room on the island, I guess I can manage," she laughed. "I'll go by and check on Skip before I come down. I want to monitor his temperature regularly, since that's a good indicator of infection. I'll go back and change those bandages just before bed time."

Sanders kissed her, briefly touching her lips with his, and held her close for a few seconds. He whispered a soft goodbye and headed down the hallway. Julie stood watching him walk away, her heart already breaking with the knowledge she would have to leave him and this beautiful island in a few short days. When he was out of sight, she let herself into her room, tears running down her cheeks.

Later that evening, after they had enjoyed Miss Marie's delicious dinner, Sanders and Julie went back to check on Skip. He was looking tired and uncomfortable with his mangled leg propped up on pillows. He found his ever-present grin however when Julie came into the room.

"Dr. Shelton, even in regular clothes you are by far the most gorgeous doctor I have ever seen!" Skip declared. "If you worked on the island, I'd have to think up mysterious illnesses just so I could come by to see you every week."

"How much of that pain medicine did you take?" Julie inquired with a smile on her face. "I'm thinking we need to decrease the dosage since you're obviously hallucinating."

"I haven't had any paid meds and I have to agree 100% with Skip," Sanders argued jokingly. "You are certainly the loveliest doctor I've ever seen. In Texas, doctors are old guys with bald heads and thick eyeglasses. Do those patients of yours in that heathen town of Chicago have any idea just how lucky they are?"

"Enough guys!" Julie declared with a blush spreading over her cheeks. "It's hard to be professional with you two embarrassing me like this."

She shooed Sanders out of the way and worked swiftly, changing bandages on Skip's arms and legs. With that task complete, she put ointment on the worst of the road burn abrasions and then took his temperature. Everything was looking good, but the tension in his eyes told her he was in a good bit of pain.

"Here's a pain pill. That should help you sleep," Julie smiled as she handed him a glass of water. "If you wake up in pain later tonight, you can take another one in six hours. So anytime after three o'clock will work. Just be sure to note the time so you don't take them too close together. If you need anything during the night, call my room. I'm a doctor so middle of the night calls don't bother me much."

"Skip, there are two people on the late shift tonight," Sanders noted. "One will work the desk and one will stay up here with you. I think that's best until you're back on your feet. They have instructions that you are not to be left alone under any circumstances. Oh, before I forget, Captain Hall from the local police will be by in the morning to talk to you. He needs a statement about your accident."

"Dr. Shelton, Mr. Sanders, I don't know what to say," Skip said quietly, his eyes already beginning to droop. "You two are awesome. Thank you so much for everything."

Skip quickly drifted off and Julie and Sanders stayed until Mitzi, one of the night shift employees showed up. With instructions on patient care given, they walked back to Julie's room. When they reached the door, Julie turned around and looked into his eyes.

"I need to sleep here tonight in case Skip needs me. Can you stay?" she asked with a hint of anxiety.

"You couldn't keep me away," he answered, his eyes black with passion. "I only have you for a few more days and I intend to enjoy those days to the fullest."

He leaned over and touched his lips to hers. The electricity that sizzled between them with that single kiss ignited a fire in both of them. By the time they were through the door, their clothes were being discarded on the floor. Seconds later, they were both naked and locked in an embrace that turned the fire into a raging inferno.

Sanders was frantic to be inside her and he couldn't take the time to move them to the bed. He had to have her right now. His skin was burning where her breasts were pressing against him. His rock hard penis was throbbing where it was pressing against her stomach. If he wasn't inside her in seconds, he knew he would die from need.

He lifted her up and Julie straddled him, wrapping her arms around his neck and her legs around his waist as he pushed her back against the door. He moved his hips back until his penis was poised to enter her. He had a brief thought that he should be sure she was ready but it vanished when she licked his ear and begged him to take her.

The sound of her voice pleading for him sent Sanders totally out of control. He plunged his hard penis into her and began thrusting in and out with abandon. He couldn't think, couldn't do anything

112

except press her to the door and push himself into her heat and wetness.

God, she was wet, coming again and again, her juices running over his balls and dripping down his legs. Julie's arms were tight around his neck, her tongue in his mouth, and her breasts mashed against his chest as his thrusting grew even harder. She put her feet on his ass and pushed him deeper and deeper into her. She was grinding her clit against his pelvic bone, moaning as she came over and over.

She was completely out of control now. Julie's mind was unable to comprehend a single thought as her body convulsed and her pussy tightened around him. She rode him hard until he was as out of control as she was. She held him tight against her with her legs and arms as his thrusting became even harder and deeper.

Sanders fought his rising orgasm but he was too far gone. He shoved his hardness deep into her one last time, groaning out her name as he came with a ferocious roar. She screamed his name as the last thrust sent her spiraling over the edge once more to an orgasm of unbelievable heights.

They remained entwined for several minutes, Julie pressed against the door, Sanders leaning against her. When he was finally able to breathe, he carried her ten steps to the bed, his partially erect penis still inside her. He was getting ready to lay her down when she clutched her arms and legs tightly around him again and cried out, another orgasm racing through her body. He felt her spasm around his penis and, to his total amazement, he was immediately rock hard again. He laid her back on the bed, her legs still locked around his waist. He began to thrust uncontrollably into her and in seconds, they both came once more, crying out the other's name in unison.

Many hours later Julie woke to find herself wrapped in Sanders' arms. She had never felt so at peace, never felt that anything in her life was as right as this. She luxuriated in the moment. Reality could wait until another day.

CHAPTER 12

The next morning as Julie was checking Skip's bandages, a knock sounded at the door. She opened the door to find Captain Hall standing there. Smiling, Julie let him in.

"Good morning Captain Hall," she said. "How are you this beautiful morning?"

"Good, thank you, Dr. Shelton," he replied. "How's your patient doing? Sanders said he thought Skip was up to a short interview but you have the final say."

"I think he's up to it. He has even more reason than I do to want these people found. If I think he's getting too tired, I'll let you know."

They crossed the room and Julie introduced the police captain to Skip. Skip had told Julie that he had seen Captain Hall on the island but had never been introduced before now.

"I'm glad to see you're healing," Captain Hall began. "Can you tell me what happened the other night? I don't know if you remember but I was there with Sanders when you were found by the roadside. I have an idea of what went on but need a formal statement from you."

"I left the hotel just before eleven o'clock that night," Skip said. "I finished my last snorkel tour about six o'clock and was hanging out at the bar, talking to Alex. I was biking home on Guy Banks like I always do. I live in a little house just at the north end of road with a couple of other guys who also work here. When I was about halfway

115

across, I heard a car but didn't see any lights. The way the trees grow over the road kind of distorts the sound and I wasn't sure which way it was coming from. I thought it was coming from the north so I made sure I was off to the side of the southbound lane."

Skip stopped to take a drink of water, looking flushed and a little wild-eyed. Julie looked at him and quietly asked if he was OK to continue. He shook his head yes and went on.

"I was sitting on my bike on the side of the road trying to figure out where the car was when all of the sudden the headlights came on behind me. I guess it was coming from the south after all. In a second, I realized it was coming straight at me. I tried to move further off the road but it was coming too fast. Next thing I knew, I was flying through the air and I landed in the middle of the road. The car stopped with the headlights shining on me and two guys got out. They came over and I thought they were going to help me. Oh God, I was in such pain."

He stopped again and took another sip of water. Julie was becoming concerned that he was getting too agitated, but knew this was really important. She was also getting scared because it sounded so close to what happened to her.

"Anyway," Skip continued. "The first guy rolled me onto my back and told the second guy not to worry, that I was alive but probably not for long. The second guy began digging into my pockets. He took all of my tips for the day and my wallet. That really made me mad because I had over $400 in tips....the most I've ever made! Then they just walked away, laughing about how I wouldn't make it through the night."

Once more Skip stopped and Julie could see tears in his eyes. She understood his fear and her heart went out to him. She sat on the side of his bed and held his hand.

"I know how scared you were," she said. "These same guys tried to run me down the other day. I was just lucky that they didn't hit me. Can you go on? Captain Hall needs as much information as possible so he can get them."

Skip looked at Julie, took a deep breath, and continued.

"I knew if I laid in the middle of the road I would get run over for sure, so I pulled myself over to where my bike was on the side of the road. I didn't think I would ever get there with my leg twisted backward and useless. I just kept pulling myself along with my arms until I got to the bike. It was so crushed and mangled, I wasn't sure it was my bike when I reached it. Once I got off the road, I must have passed out. The next thing I knew, Mr. Sanders was shaking my shoulder."

"Could you tell what kind of vehicle they were driving?" the captain asked.

"It was small but not a car. Maybe a jeep? I don't know for sure…it was so dark and I was in so much pain," Skip said, his voice quivering with emotion. "I wish I could give you a license plate number or something like they do in the movies. But it was just too damn dark!"

"That's OK," Captain Hall said. "Your story sounds very much like what happened to Dr.

Shelton. The vehicle you both saw also sounds very much like the one reported by two other people who have been robbed. So far you're the only one who actually got a good look at the men. Do you think you could identify either man?"

"It was dark and I was in shock, but with the headlights shining on them, I got a decent look. I don't know…..I might be able to identify them. I'll certainly try," Skip ventured. "I'll never forget their voices though. Joking and laughing about how I was gonna die in the road. Put them in a room and have them talk, I'll be able to tell you for sure!"

Julie could see that Skip was getting very agitated now and his tight face was giving away the amount of pain he was in. As a victim, she wanted to pull every single detail from Skip's brain, but as a doctor she had to protect him. That meant calling a halt to the interview. Skip obviously needed some pain medication and more rest.

"Captain Hall," she interrupted. "I think that's about all he can take today. He needs some pain meds and needs to sleep for awhile. Maybe you can come back tomorrow if you need more from him."

"That's enough for now," the captain responded. "I'm convinced the four incidents we have had are all by the same two guys. Now I need to figure out where they're hiding and take them down. When I find them, we'll do a voice ID with Skip and see if any of you can ID the vehicle."

Something suddenly came to Julie's conscious mind. She jumped up and paced around the room. Both men watched her as a wave of emotions crossed her face.

"Are you OK Dr. Shelton?" Captain Hall inquired.

"I just remembered something," she replied. "When the jeep was coming towards me, I noticed that there was paint or something on the front bumper and the bumper was sitting at an odd angle. The paint was light colored against the green jeep. Maybe yellow or beige?"

"My bike is yellow!" Skip exclaimed. "It has to be the same guys!"

"Between this information, the information from the other victims, and my gut feeling, I know it's the same guys," Captain Hall said firmly. "I'll find that jeep and those guys will be spending their time in jail if I have anything to do with it."

"Now I have to insist that you go Captain," Julie said in her most authoritative doctor's voice. "Skip needs some pain pills and he needs to rest."

"You better listen to her, Howie," a voice called from the doorway.

Three heads turned to see Sanders entering the room. They had been so engrossed in Skip's tale that they hadn't heard the door open.

"If you don't listen, I can't be held responsible when she physically removes you from the room," he laughed. "I'd be willing to bet she is one protective momma bear when it comes to her patients."

"And you would win that bet Sanders," Julie answered with a smile. "Now both of you out of here while I get Skip settled! Go!"

Both men headed towards the door talking in low voices about what Skip had just told them. Julie bustled about getting Skip's pain medication and rearranging his injured leg on plumped pillows. As the men started out the door Sanders turned and spoke.

"When you finish up here Julie, stop down by the desk please. I'll wait for you there."

Julie nodded an OK and continued getting her patient settled as the door shut. She put some salve on Skip's abrasions and made sure he had water and a phone within reach.

"Need anything else before I go?" she asked.

"Not that I can think of," Skip replied. "But can I ask you a question?"

"Sure, anything for you," she said with a big smile. "If I remember correctly you saved me from drowning so I owe you big time. That means free medical care while I'm here and answers to all of your questions."

"We were just wondering....well, me and some of the other hotel employees....we wondered if you and Mr. Sanders were, you know, a couple when he was in Texas," Skip stammered, suddenly embarrassed by his question.

"Oh, uh, no," Julie stuttered turning a deep red. "I met him on the beach the first night I was here."

"Oh, we just figured that maybe you knew each other before. I mean he never has dinner with the guests or takes them out kayaking or anything. Actually the girls at the reception desk say they've

120

never seen him take a woman to his apartment before. I guess he must really like you," he finished.

"I guess he must," she replied, surprised that her affair with Sanders was so obvious to his employees. "Any other questions before I go?"

"No, but we all like you and wish you would stay," Skip responded. "It would be so awesome if you could be the doctor at the new medical center."

"Thank you for the nice compliment but I have an office full of patients waiting for me back in Chicago," Julie remarked. "I have to get back to them when my vacation is over. And you have to get some rest. I see your eyes drooping already. I'll check on you again this evening, but don't hesitate to have the front desk find me if you need me."

"OK Doc," he muttered as his eyes closed.

Julie left Skip to his nap and headed down to the reception area. She saw Sanders standing off to one side talking to Captain Hall. He looked up, saw her, and motioned her over.

"Howie was just telling me that Skip might be able to identify these guys. He also said you remembered that the vehicle they were driving had paint on the bumper."

"It just came to me when Skip was talking about his ordeal," she answered. "I'm sure I can identify the jeep if it's found. Seeing how badly hurt he is and hearing him tell about these guys laughing that he might die, I want to do anything I can to help put them away."

"Dr. Shelton," Captain Hall began. "Since you and Skip can both help ID them, I suggest you be very careful until they are caught. If they will purposely run down innocent people, there's no telling what else they might do."

"Don't worry about that Howie," Sanders interrupted. "I won't let her out of my sight for the rest of her stay here. I also hired a security company to put guards on duty 24/7, roaming around the hotel to look out for anyone who doesn't belong. They will be instructed to ask anyone suspicious wandering around the halls to show their room keycard."

"I think that's a really good idea considering what happened last night," the police captain noted.

"What happened last night?" Julie asked, suddenly afraid.

"I'll let Sanders tell you." Captain Hall said. "I need to get back to the station and organize my officers and some volunteers to start a sweep of the island. We have to find that jeep and when we do, we'll find those guys."

The two men shook hands and goodbyes were said. Captain Hall strode out of the hotel, leaving Julie looking at Sanders, her eyes full of questions.

"There was another robbery last night," he started before she could ask. "This time they hit a man who had $10,000 in his pocket. He had just come back from the casino on Grand Cayman and was bragging to his pals on the shuttle boat that he hit the big time payoff on the slots. When he went up to his room at Paradise Villas, they ambushed him, shoved him inside, and robbed him. The guest next door heard him yelling late last night. It looks like the robbers tied him up and knocked him out.

When he came to, he started screaming to high heaven. Thank God he wasn't staying here!"

"This is getting very scary Sanders," Julie stuttered. "The robbers must have heard him bragging on the boat from Grand Cayman. How else would they have known about the money?"

"Well now Darlin', that's the question Howie and I were mulling over when you got here," Sanders responded. "It's certainly like they have someone on the inside somewhere. However, having someone inside here and someone inside at Paradise Villas doesn't make sense. That would mean a lot of people are in on it. It's just very odd. The first two robberies appear to be spur of the moment. They happened after dark on the beach and netted small sums. Skip's however seems to be planned just like last night's. And honestly, I'm just not sure about what happened to you."

"There's no way they could have planned to run me off the road," she commented. "I didn't know until I was at the beach at Bloody Bay that I was going to come back that way."

"Maybe it was another spur of the moment thing, but they tried to run over you," he exclaimed. "And now you can ID their car. I meant what I said to Howie. I'm not letting you out of my sight until you head back to Chicago."

Sanders pulled Julie to him and held her tight. She put her arms around him and snuggled into his chest. Neither of them saw the Sunset Inn employee standing behind the large palm tree, listening to their conversation.

When they broke the embrace, Sanders told
Julie that he had plans for them for the afternoon.
However, he had some hotel business to take care of
first. He headed for the hotel office, leaving her on
her own. Julie changed into her bikini and then went
to the pool to wait for him.

An hour later, they took off in the hotel's
LandRover for Point of Sand Beach. Point of Sand
was at the far eastern tip of the island. Sanders told
her that the beach was too far for biking, especially
in the afternoon heat. Julie wasn't convinced by his
argument. She was sure the reason was to keep her
from being an easy target on a bike. Now that it was
known that she and Skip had talked to the police,
Sanders protective instincts were in overdrive.

When they arrived, Julie was stunned by the
beautiful vista before her. The white sand beach and
clear turquoise water left her speechless. She could
stand at the water's edge and see the coral reef
teeming with fish and other sea creatures. Across
the water she could see Cayman Brac shimmering in
the afternoon sun.

"This beach is almost as beautiful as the one
on Owens Island," she whispered, her wide eyes
scanning back and forth. "I didn't know there could
be this much beauty in such a small place."

"You've barely made a dent in the amazing
sights of Little Cayman," Sanders teased. "But I'll
do my best to make sure you get to see them all in
the next week. It's the least I can do since your
vacation hasn't exactly been totally relaxing."

Julie turned to him and gave him a blinding
smile.

"I know it hasn't been perfect but I wouldn't change a thing. This is the best vacation I've ever had!" she declared.

"Robbers running around, my best snorkel instructor in bed with a broken leg, and an esteemed doctor from Chicago run down by the same nuts who broke my employee's leg. Wow, you must have had some really bad vacations in the past!" Sanders laughed.

"OK, I might change a thing or two," she conceded. "But not everything. I wouldn't change the beauty of this island or the time we spent together. Those are both priceless to me."

"And to me too," he replied. "You are an amazing woman and I haven't had this much fun in years. I'm glad you chose my little hotel for your vacation."

They stood quietly at the water's edge for a few minutes, both of them drinking in the healing power of the sun, sand, and ocean. Finally Julie broke the spell, splashing Sanders and then racing into the water.

"Bet you can't catch me!" she cried.

"Bet I can!" he yelled as he dove in after her.

With two long strokes he reached her and pulled her under. Julie was ready for him and scrambled out of his grasp before her head went under the water. They spent the next few hours swimming, floating, and enjoying the warm ocean water. Sanders was sitting in the shallow water when he realized it was getting close to sunset. As he gazed around, he saw that they were alone. Julie was sitting beside him looking tanned, gorgeous, and serene. The worry he had seen over Skip and the bandits was no longer visible on her beautiful face.

"Hey, come here," he said in a soft voice. "I could sure use a kiss right about now."

"Oh yeah?" she said with a mischievous grin. "Why should I give you a kiss?"

"Because I'm handsome, sexy, and an excellent kisser," he responded, his eyes crinkling with humor. "Besides, I have the keys to the car and you need a ride back to the hotel."

"Hmmmm, blackmail," she said shaking her head. "Well, I guess I have to give you a kiss because I wouldn't want to have to call your buddy Howie for a ride. He's pretty busy today."

Julie leaned over and put her lips against his. Sanders' tongue caressed her lips and then slid into her mouth. Her body was instantly on fire and she felt an overwhelming need to have him inside her. When his hand slid under her bikini top and his fingers pinched her nipple, she moaned and shivered. She wanted him so badly she could barely form a coherent thought. He pulled her closer and put his other hand on the small of her back.

"Sit on my lap, Darlin'," he murmured against her lips.

She straddled him and gasped as he slid his hand down the back of her bikini bottoms. His fingers caressed first one cheek then the other while he kissed her lips and her neck. His other hand left her breast to untie the bikini top. He moved it out of the way so he could gaze at her swollen breasts and then his mouth was sucking her nipples, one after the other, making her squirm and moan. He now had

126

both hands under the water, caressing her butt and pressing her against his growing erection.

"I need you," she whispered, her mouth against his ear. "Please, I need you inside me."

Sanders knew that he was in heaven. This astounding woman was sitting on his lap in shallow water moaning at his touch. Her nipples were hard little rocks in his mouth. His hands fit perfectly on her ass, like her cheeks were made for them. His passion was burning him up from the inside. He had never wanted a woman so much and in so many ways. When she whispered "I need you", he thought he would explode right then. He removed his mouth from her nipples and looked into her eyes. The arousal he saw, the raw need, was the most potent aphrodisiac one could ever imagine. He needed to be inside her as much as she needed him.

He slid her back just enough to release his rock hard penis from his swim trunks. Then he slid her forward again, pulled the crotch of her bikini bottoms to the side, and plunged into her heat. Oh God she was so wet, so ready, so damn hot inside. Julie cried out when he entered her and she instinctively locked her legs around his waist. She put her arms around his neck, pressed her breasts against his chest, and pulled his mouth to hers. She hungrily sucked on his tongue while he pushed up into her. After only a few thrusts, she threw her head back and moaned as a shattering orgasm took over her body.

He continued to stroke her with his hard, hot penis, fighting for control as her nipples burned holes in his chest. She came again and again and again, each orgasm stronger than the one before it. Her pussy was gripping him as her muscles contracted over and over and he was soon at the point of no return. He grabbed her hips under the water and pulled her tight against him. With a huge groan, his body jerked up, pushing his penis deep into her super heated pussy and he came, calling out her name. His final thrust pushed her over the edge and she screamed, blinded by an orgasm so strong her body went completely stiff, then totally limp.

She lay against his chest gasping for breath. He too was gasping and his heart felt like it was going to explode from his chest. They sat entwined in the water as the sky turned red and orange with the setting sun. Finally Sanders spoke.

"We need to get out of the water Darlin'," he said. "The underwater predators come out at night. Even more important, I have sand in my shorts and it's not feeling too good."

Julie laughed and kissed him. She had never been so sexually sated or so happy.

CHAPTER 13

The last week of Julie's vacation took on a routine that she had never expected. Mornings she spent jogging with Sanders and then taking care of Skip, checking his wounds and helping him with therapy to keep his muscles toned while his leg healed. If she had time, she would swim laps at the pool or have an iced tea at the tiki bar. Sanders spent the mornings taking care of his responsibilities at the hotel. He had a good Housekeeping Manager, Miss Marie ran the kitchen staff, and his front desk clerks were the cream of the crop. He managed the day-to-day operations, personnel issues, and worked directly with his accountant on financial issues. Fortunately this left him with time each day to devote to Julie.

They spent the afternoons exploring the island and each other. Julie felt fortunate to have such a knowledgeable and sexy guide to show her parts of the island she may not have visited otherwise. They saw the normal tourist spots like the Little Cayman Museum. It contained a treasure trove of artifacts from the time when Little Cayman was an unknown island with only a few local inhabitants. They also went to the Booby Pond Nature Reserve. With the telescopes on the observation deck at the Nature Preserve, they could see flocks of Red Footed Boobies nesting in the mangroves. They could also see the surrounding ocean for miles. It was a sight that took Julie's breath away.

129

Since Sanders had a more intimate knowledge of the island, he also took her to some local favorite spots that most tourists never found. They explored Sparrowhawk Hill, Weary Hill, and Snipe Point. They drove on little known dirt tracks through the island's forests to visit with locals who obviously knew and loved Sanders. These afternoons were Julie's favorites. While she enjoyed the tourist spots, the more isolated places gave her an understanding of Sanders' deep love of the island and the people who had adopted him into their family.

Each time they stopped at a small cabin off the main road, Sanders and Julie were warmly welcomed and invited in to share a cup of coffee or a meal. The new medical clinic was a topic of discussion at every stop. The Little Cayman locals were excited to know they would have medical care in easy reach and exceedingly grateful to Sanders for providing it. When the talk turned to staffing a doctor at the clinic, Sanders would quickly steer the conversation to something else. It was a subject he didn't want to discuss in front of Julie.

On the Wednesday of that last week, they stopped to see an elderly lady whose grandson worked in the hotel kitchen with Miss Marie. Granny Lele was a ninety year-old black woman whose wrinkled skin and tiny frame belied her strength. Granny, as all the locals called her, invited them to have a glass of iced tea on her wide front porch. She began to talk and told Julie she had been born here and had lived on Little Cayman her entire life. Her ancestors had migrated from the island of

Trinidad more than one hundred years earlier. She looked fondly at Sanders and then turned back to Julie.

"When the other hotels opened, the owners recruited workers from distant countries with promises of good wages and a beautiful place to live. Sanders looked first to the locals to staff his hotel," Granny Lele told her. "He has taken us into his trust and in return we have taken him into our family. I'm afraid without him we might have died off. All the young folk wanted to leave the island but now they have a reason to stay."

She turned to look at Sanders with her rheumy eyes and pointed a finger at him.

"I hear there be some bad things happening around the island and at your place," she said. "My Tommy says the pretty lady doctor here and that sweet boy Skip were attacked. What are you doing to find these hooligans?"

"Tommy is Granny's grandson," Sanders told Julie. Then looking at Granny Lele, he continued: "We're working closely with Captain Hall. He is the police chief, if you remember, and he's doing everything he can to find these guys."

"I may be old but I'm not senile yet!" the old lady snapped. "I know Captain Hall is looking into it but I figured since your lady friend was involved you would take a bigger interest in the hunt. But then maybe I misunderstood what I heard about you two." A gap toothed grin spread across her face and she cackled quietly to herself.

"Now Granny, I don't know what you heard but I'm looking after Julie. She doesn't go far from the hotel without me," Sanders said, his face turning crimson. "I have Skip in a room at the hotel until he is well enough to go home. Both Julie and Skip have talked to Howie, and he's convinced all the troubles of the last few weeks are the work of the same two or three guys. He's bringing in some outside help to scour the island in a day or so. You can count on me being part of that search party."

The old lady turned toward Julie and studied her for a moment. Julie became uncomfortable under her scrutiny and began to squirm a little in her chair.

"I was beginning to wonder if Sanders was ever going to find a woman his equal, but from what I'm hearing, you just might fit that bill," Granny Lele began. "Not only are you young and pretty, but I hear you can hold your own when he tries to bully you. And you being a doctor is perfect. I always wanted a woman doctor and with you at the medical clinic, I'll finally get my wish."

"Oh no," Julie hurriedly interrupted before this went any farther. "I'm just down here on vacation. I have my own practice up in Chicago. Actually, I'm leaving on Saturday."

The truth of what she had just said hit Julie like a ton of bricks. Two more days and she would be headed back home, headed back to a life without the most interesting, exciting man she had ever known. How would she ever survive? She looked up to see the old woman staring at her as if she could read her mind.

"Of course you're going back to Chicago," Granny said with a knowing look. She turned to

Sanders. "You know, I raised my Tommy from the time he was a tiny baby. His momma died shortly after he was born. I know him inside out and something is bothering him. He won't talk about whatever it is, but I got a feeling he knows something about what's going on. Maybe if you talk to him......."

"I sure will Granny. If he knows something, we need to get that info to Howie," Sanders answered as he rose from his seat. "I'd love to stay and chat some more but we really need to go. The hotel doesn't run itself and Julie needs to look in on Skip. Thanks for the iced tea."

Sanders and Julie said goodbye and headed down the steps. Granny Lele rose from her seat too and walked to the steps.

"Only a stupid man would let that one go," she said, nodding her head at Julie. "I never took you for a stupid man, Sanders."

With that she turned and went back inside her little house. Sanders tried to ignore what Granny had said, but black thoughts were already swirling in his head. He had been trying to pretend that Julie was never leaving. Hearing her say it out loud had felt like a rock slamming into his heart. He couldn't bear the idea that in two more days she would be gone from his life. Unfortunately, she had seemed very anxious to make sure Granny knew she was leaving.

The ride back to the hotel was a little awkward. They exchanged small talk about Granny and how she ruled most of the locals on the island. They speculated on what Tommy might know. But neither talked about the six-hundred pound elephant sitting in the car with them.....the fact that their time together was now very short. When they arrived, Sanders told Julie he needed to check with the front desk to see if there was anything urgent, but he asked her to wait before she went up to see Skip. When he finished, he took her hand and walked her down the hallway to his apartment.

As soon as they entered the apartment, they came together as if drawn by a silent magnetic force. The electricity between them seemed to have exploded with the open acknowledgement that their affair was almost over. The first kiss sent shivers down Julie's spine and she wrapped her arms around his neck. His tongue was immediately in her mouth and his hands frantically removed her top and her shorts. She wasn't wearing a bra and his fingers caressed her nipples until they were hard. He could feel her breasts swelling in his hands as her arousal rose. He knew she was wet and he wanted to taste her, but she was holding on to him and sucking on his tongue like she would never let go. He finally broke the embrace and began kissing her neck as he slid her panties over her hips and let them drop to the floor.

They were standing in the entryway, next to his small kitchen area. Sanders lifted Julie and sat her on the cool granite top of the kitchen island. He told her to lay back and he placed her legs over his shoulders. He groaned as he saw the wetness glistening at her pussy lips and he spread her legs wider needing to lick every last drop from her. He leaned down and blew hot breath on her clit, causing

her to moan and grab the edges of the countertop.
His tongue flicked out and the tip tickled her hard
clit in short little jabs. Julie moaned again and
arched up toward his mouth. He ran his tongue over
her pussy lips and clit in a slow, dragging motion as
he grabbed her hips with both hands. He pulled her
tight against his mouth and began lapping up her
juices as she writhed and moaned louder.

Julie was sure this was the most erotic feeling
in the world. The cold granite against her back
contrasted sharply with the extreme heat inside her
body. She could feel a huge orgasm building....one
that would take over her entire body. Sanders
continued to slide his incredible tongue in and out of
her with a swipe across her clit every now and then.
Her butt was raised off the countertop as he held her
against his mouth and she grabbed the sides of the
counter as the first wave hit her. She called out his
name as the orgasm roared through her body. Her
legs involuntarily squeezed together and she could
feel his hair rubbing the inside of her thighs as he
continued to assault her pussy and clit with his
tongue. Instead of subsiding, the orgasm grew in
intensity until she was coming nonstop. Her pussy
was in spasms and she had a brief feeling of wetness
running down her butt cheeks.

After what seemed like hours, Sanders lifted
his head and looked at Julie. Her body was still in
the throes of orgasm and the sight of her face while
she came set him on fire. He touched her clit with
his thumb and she screamed and arched up higher
and higher. He touched her again and watched as the
wetness ran out of her pussy and dripped down her

butt crack. He looked up and saw that her eyes were fixed on him now. He continued to play his thumb against her clit and stared into her eyes as she came again and again. He could feel his hard penis straining against his shorts and wanted to be in her so bad it hurt. However, he also wanted to push her higher and higher. He wanted her to think about him when she was back in Chicago and remember him as the man who took her where no one else could.

Finally Julie closed her eyes and moaned "stop, oh God stop" and Sanders moved his hand away. She lay back on the granite counter and tried to regain her breath. He watched her breasts move up and down with each giant breath she struggled to take. Knowing her wild and uninhibited response was his "fault" turned him on more than he knew was possible. He had to be inside her, right now. She opened her eyes and looked directly into his. He knew without words that she wanted him inside her almost as much as he did. He pulled her up from the countertop and held her against him.

"Let's go to the bedroom," he whispered. "I need to be inside you so bad Darlin'."

"Can't walk," she panted, still trying to regain her breath.

Sanders picked her up and carried her into the bedroom. He laid her gently on the bed and quickly stripped naked. His penis sprung out, hard and throbbing, when he dropped his shorts to the floor. She looked at it and then at him, the most erotic smile on her face that he had ever seen.

"Take me Sanders," Julie whispered. "I need you. God I need you so bad."

CAYMAN KISS

He climbed onto the bed and moved between her spread legs. His penis rubbed against her thigh and he groaned with need. He grabbed it in his hand and rubbed the tip against her dripping wet pussy lips, then against her clit. She moaned and shuddered as she came again. He could stand it no longer and plunged into her. Her legs spread wider, taking him deeper into the heated core of her body. He began stroking her, pulling almost all the way out and then pushing back into her, deeper and deeper. He lowered his upper body to hers, her hard nipples burning into his chest.

She put her arms around him and pulled him tight against her chest. Her lips touched his and her pelvis arched up as she came again. He licked her lips with his tongue and slid it into her waiting mouth. She tasted herself on his tongue and groaned. The kiss was hot and sensual, sending both of them perilously close to the edge. Without realizing it, Sanders set a rhythm with his tongue and his penis. His tongue was sliding in when his penis slid partially out. His penis was sliding in when his tongue slid out. They rocked back and forth, locked together in an embrace that had their bodies pressed tightly together from lips to pelvis.

Julie pulled her mouth away as a scream of pure pleasure escaped her lips. She had an orgasm that consumed her entire body in a way she had never before felt. Sanders felt her tighten around his hard shaft and then felt her juices gushing over him, heard her say his name as she crashed over the edge. It was all he could take. He groaned, called her name, and came so intensely he was sure he would

137

pass out. When he had nothing left in him, he collapsed on top of her.

They lay fully entwined for a long time. Finally, Sanders rolled off her and pulled her onto his shoulder. Neither could speak, their bodies drained and exhausted. Julie was almost asleep when he moved slightly and spoke in a whisper.

"I don't know what I'm going to do when you're gone," he said in a voice strangled by emotion.

Julie wasn't sure she had heard him right but didn't want to spoil the moment by asking him to repeat himself. If she hadn't heard correctly, she didn't really want to know anyway because she was thinking the exact same thing.

CHAPTER 14

On Thursday morning, with only two days remaining of her vacation, Julie and Sanders shared breakfast in his apartment. As he went to the kitchen to get more coffee, he ran his hand over the countertop of the kitchen island. He turned, smiled at her, and then began to chuckle.

"I can honestly say I will never look at this kitchen island in the same way again," he said with a wicked gleam in his eye. "And if I had time, there would be a repeat performance right here this morning."

"I think your performance in the bedroom last night and again early this morning was pretty amazing," Julie said with an equally wicked gleam in her eyes. "I can't imagine you're ready to go again."

"Darlin' where you're concerned, I'm *always* ready," he drawled. "Now I'd better get out of here or I'll never get any work done today. I'll be talking to Tommy later. If Granny Lele thinks he's holding something in, then he probably is. I'll look for you when I'm ready and let you sit in."

He kissed her and quickly left, walking a little awkwardly due to his partially erect penis. Julie went upstairs to her room and showered. She dressed in shorts, a tank top, and canvas sneakers. As an afterthought she put her seahorse necklace on. She remembered Sanders staring at her breasts when she had worn it before and blushed as the thought sent heat waves through her body. She laid out her bathing suit and got her backpack ready for their trip to the other side of the island that afternoon. Her tasks completed, she headed down the hall to Skip's room. She knocked on the door and it was opened by a hotel staffer she didn't recognize. He stepped back without speaking, letting her into the room.

"Hi Skip! How's my favorite patient today?" she asked as she crossed the room.

"Better, much better, Dr. Shelton," he giggled. "No middle of the night pain pills last night. How's that for improvement? And wow, you look extra beautiful today! Cool necklace pretty doctor. It looks really good the way it falls in between....ooops better shut up now!!"

"Sounds like someone is in a really good mood today," Julie replied with a smile at her patient who was obviously feeling no pain. "I'm glad your pain level is decreasing. Let me take a look at the abrasions that are still healing and then we can do some physical therapy for your leg. After that you may need a pain pill so don't hesitate to take one if necessary. By the way, are you going to introduce me to this morning's babysitter?"

"Oh, sorry Dr. Shelton," Skip answered with another giggle. "Andrew, this is Dr. Shelton. She's my angel and my hero as well as the best doctor on the island. Dr. Shelton, this is Andrew. He works in the kitchen with Miss Marie and Tommy."

"Nice to meet you doc," Andrew said. "I hear from Skip that not only have you been taking care of him but you had a close call too. I bet that was pretty scary."

"It sure was, Andrew, but I was much luckier than Skip," Julie noted with a shudder. "Those

140

horrible men took off after they ran me off the road. I don't even want to think about what might have happened if they had backed up."

"Wow, did you get a good look at them?" Andrew asked, staring intently at Julie. "Do you think you could identify them?"

"I doubt I can identify them, but I'm sure I can identify their car," Julie replied, her attention focused on Skip's bandages. "Skip saw their faces so I think between the two of us we can nail them when Captain Hall finds them."

"Does he know where they are yet?" Andrew questioned. "I mean, does he have any good clues?"

Julie stopped what she was doing and turned to look at Andrew. His curiosity had her somewhat unnerved. She turned back to Skip thinking she was getting way too jumpy these days. She continued changing his bandages and noticed his eyes were beginning to droop.

"I really don't know much of anything," she said. "Everyone is cooperating with the police to get these barbarians. I am sure of one thing. They will be found and prosecuted. Captain Hall and Mr. Sanders will not be satisfied with anything else."

"Do you think they will want you to come back and testify if there's a trial? I mean you did see their jeep after all," Andrew returned in a rush. "Surely they will need a witness other than Skip."

Julie was suddenly unsettled by Andrew's questions but she did not look up from the bandage she was wrapping around Skip's upper arm. She thought carefully while she completed the task and was sure she had not told Andrew what kind of car had tried to hit her. Now how did he know it was a jeep? As far as she knew, the police hadn't released that detail.

"I have no idea what will happen," she said slowly. "Well it looks like Skip needs some sleep. He seems to have nodded off while I was changing his bandages. Why don't you and I leave him to sleep and I'll come back later for his physical therapy."

Wanting to get out of the room and away from Andrew quickly, Julie walked to the door and held it open. She didn't want to be in here with him, but she didn't want to leave him here with Skip either. Something was off and she was a little afraid of this odd young man. Andrew walked toward the door, smiling at her intently once again. As he moved into the hallway, she closed the door quietly.

"Skip sure crashed fast," Andrew said as they walked toward the elevator. "Wonder why?"

"His body is still in recovery mode," Julie replied. "He needs plenty of sleep."

"Or maybe it was the three pain pills I put in his juice before you got there," he said in a menacing tone. "He was complaining about how thirsty he was and drank all of it right down, not even realizing it was spiked. Of course this was right after he told me that you come by about the same time every morning to check on him. The exact information I needed."

Before she could react to this news, Andrew grabbed Julie around the neck and put his hand over her mouth. He pulled her roughly toward the stairwell door. Before they reached it, the door opened and two young men came into the hall. One was tall and dark haired and looked like a body builder. The other was short and squat with a shaved head. The dead look in their eyes scared Julie into total silence. They quickly pulled her into the stairwell and pushed her against the wall.

"Stay quiet Doc and we won't hurt you," the taller man growled. "Open your mouth and make a single sound and Skip will find out what it feels like to have his leg broken again. I'll personally break it with my bare hands. And then it will be your turn."

Julie nodded her understanding and Andrew removed his hand from her mouth. Even though she hadn't seen them, she knew these were the guys from the jeep and Andrew was the inside link Captain Hall was looking for. She didn't know what their intentions were but she knew she had to keep them away from Skip. She also knew she somehow had to alert a hotel staffer that she was in trouble.

The three men hustled Julie down the stairs. Instead of going out the lobby door at the bottom of the stairs, they went down a short hallway and out to the back lot of the hotel. They crossed the pavement to a beat up old car parked by the trash dumpster. The short man opened the back door and tried to push her into the car. Julie resisted and they struggled for a few seconds until he overpowered her and pushed her into the back seat. The tall man and Andrew got in the front seat. The short squat man sat down next to her and pushed her down to the floor so her head was below window level.

"Hurry up and let's get out of here," he shouted at Andrew who had taken the drivers seat.

"We have our insurance policy now and can get off this God forsaken island without a hitch."

As they screeched out of the parking lot, he turned to look at Julie and she was overcome with a terror she did not know was possible. His eyes were dead and cold and she could see violence written all over his face.

"Well pretty doctor, looks like you're in quite a pickle now aren't you?" he said in a voice that sent a shiver of dread up Julie's spine. "But don't worry, once we're safely away, we'll let you go. I just hope you're a good swimmer!"

All three men began laughing at that remark as they sped up Guy Banks Road and made a sharp left onto Olivine Kirk Drive. With the sun blocked out by the trees, Julie was suddenly in darkness as she sat shaking in fear. She could only hope someone would miss her soon and start a search. Her hand went to her neck as she fought panic and she realized her seahorse necklace was gone. Silently she prayed that Sanders would find it wherever she lost it and realize she was in trouble.

CHAPTER 15

Sanders spent the morning clearing out the giant pile of paperwork that had accumulated on his desk. He was anxious to talk to Tommy but running the hotel had to come first. When he finally got the paperwork down to a manageable level, he saw it was past lunchtime. He wondered briefly if Julie was waiting for him for lunch and decided he would find out when they spoke to Tommy. Since Tommy was his next priority, Sanders went to the kitchen to find him. He really wanted to find out what was causing Tommy enough distress that Granny Lele was worried. A part of him hoped it was about the recent robberies while another part hoped the boy wasn't involved in that mess. Whatever it was, he would get to the bottom of it. He had promised Granny Lele and he wasn't about to break a promise to the old woman.

Sanders entered the kitchen and immediately saw Miss Marie at the stove stirring something in a big pot. The smell was absolute heaven and his mouth watered. He walked up behind the cook and put his arms around her ample bulk.

"Miss Marie, will you marry me?" he asked laughing. "I would die a happy man if I had your fine food to eat every day for the rest of my life."

Miss Marie wriggled out of his grasp, shaking her head the whole time.

"Mr. Sanders I'm twenty years older than you, my hair is totally gray, and I'm as wide as I am tall," she replied with a twinkle in her eyes. "You need a young, good looking woman….like that Dr. Shelton for instance. She's pretty, smart, and very sweet. But then maybe she's too good for you!"

Miss Marie held her sides as she laughed at her own joke. Sanders laughed too but inside he was dying. The mention of Julie brought her imminent departure to mind. They had less than forty-eight hours before she would be gone for good. He wasn't sure how he would cope once she left his life forever.

"Now what are you doing in my kitchen?" Miss Marie asked, shaking a big spoon at him. "I have dinner prep to finish so I can take a much needed break. Did you miss lunch and now you've come to beg for a morsel of my good cooking?"

"Okay, Okay, I'll state my business and get out of your way," Sanders responded with a glance around the kitchen. "I did miss lunch but that's not why I'm here. I came to talk to Tommy. Granny Lele is worried about him and asked me to see if I can find out what's up with him."

"Tommy should be back soon," she announced. "I sent him off to find that shiftless Andrew. Andrew disappeared once breakfast was cooked and hasn't shown his face since. Tommy and I did all the lunch work alone. I've been meaning to talk to you about Andrew anyway. He takes off without any notice and then comes back whenever it suits him. Poor Tommy ends up doing all the clean up for one meal and the prep for the next. Mr. Sanders, I hate to complain, but I need someone who stays here and works."

"Miss Marie, I know you never complain, so Andrew must be really trying your patience," Sanders answered. "I'll talk to him as soon as I can find him. If it doesn't get better in the next few days, you let me know. And if you need someone else in here to help, just say so. I don't want my favorite chef to be overworked!"

"Wonder what got into that boy?" Miss Marie questioned with a scowl on her face. "He did real well up until a couple of weeks ago. Then he got all shifty eyed and started disappearing off and on. Tommy takes up the slack but it's just not right. I mean you're paying both of them and they should both be working."

"Don't worry, I'll find Andrew today and have a talk with him," Sanders assured her. "When Tommy comes back, can you ask him to come to my office please? If Andrew is with him, send both of them as soon as you can spare them."

Sanders went back to his office and called Julie's room but there was no answer. He checked with the front desk clerk and Alex in the tiki bar, but no one had seen her all day. He wandered past the pool but she was nowhere to be seen. A little concerned, he checked the computer, but there was no lunch charge on her room bill. He called Skip's room, but there was no answer there either. He sat at his desk and thought about what Granny Lele had said about Tommy and what Miss Marie had told him about Andrew. He began to wonder if maybe Tommy's issue was with Andrew and had nothing to do with the robberies. He was so deep in thought that the knock on his door startled him.

147

"Come in," he shouted.

When he looked up, Tommy opened the door and walked into the office.

"Were you looking for me Mr. Sanders?" Tommy inquired.

"Have a seat Tommy," Sanders began. When Tommy was settled, he continued. "I saw Granny yesterday. She's really worried about you."

"She shouldn't worry so much," Tommy replied shifting nervously in his seat. "There's nothing wrong."

"Well now, if Granny's worried, there must be something," Sanders answered, watching Tommy's face as he looked down at his feet. "Miss Marie says Andrew is slacking off lately and you're covering for him. Want to tell me about it?"

"It's nothing," Tommy said quietly. "Really, it's not a big deal."

"It's a big deal to me if one of my employees isn't pulling his weight around here," Sanders declared. "And there's obviously something going on with you or Granny wouldn't have asked me to talk to you."

Sanders continued to watch as Tommy's face took on a look of pain. He was definitely hiding something and struggling with himself about whether to tell.

"If it's not about Andrew, then what is it? Might as well spill it because we're gonna sit here until you do," Sanders drawled. "I can't go back to Granny Lele empty handed Tommy....you, of all people, should know that."

148

Tommy looked up at Sanders. His body language screamed anxiety. He ran his hands over his face and then smoothed his hair back. He sighed loudly and a look of resignation came over him.

"Andrew has been really weird the last few weeks," he began. "He slips off somewhere and is gone for an hour or two but he always comes back. I talked to him about it yesterday and he said he had some things he was taking care of but it would all be over in a few days. I asked him what kind of stuff was causing him to be gone so much, but he wouldn't tell me. He said I'm better off not knowing."

He looked at Sanders again and knew from the look on Sanders' face that this wasn't going to be enough information. He took a deep breath and continued.

"But I think I know anyway. Actually I think I need to talk to Captain Hall. I think Andrew might be mixed up with the robberies," Tommy related quietly, then continued in a rush. "I went to find him after I finished the lunch prep. He told me he wanted to go check on Skip, but no one answered when I knocked on Skip's door. I stopped to talk to Janie at the front desk on my way back to the kitchen. She said she was supposed to sit with Skip this morning, but Andrew showed up and sent her away, said he would stay. She thought that was weird since he was supposed to be working in the kitchen with me."

"Whoa, slow down son," Sanders answered. "Let's start at the beginning. I'm not getting the connection between Andrew staying with Skip and your feeling that he's mixed up in the robberies."

"Well, there's just some stuff that doesn't add up," Tommy stated vehemently, suddenly needing to come clean with his boss. "A bunch of us were hanging at the tiki bar with Alex the night Skip was hurt. Andrew was with us. Skip was bragging about how he had made over $400 in tips that day. Some old lady took a liking to him and gave him a $200 tip. Andrew disappeared for about ten minutes right after he heard that, but came back. Then when Skip left to go home, he took off again and went roaring out of the parking lot in his old beat up car. When we found out Skip had been hurt, he just kinda shrugged like it was no big deal. And he hasn't taken a turn staying with Skip, so when he said he was going up there it was just strange."

Tommy stopped and looked at Sanders again. He was scared, terrified of something. He took another deep breath and started talking again.

"I know that by itself isn't much but then there was the day he was off and went to Grand Cayman. He came back on the shuttle boat early in the evening. He came to the hotel and was hanging out at the tiki bar again. He had a couple of drinks and started talking to me about this guy on the boat who had won $10,000 on a slot machine at one of the casinos. He was saying with that much money he could blow this place and go somewhere that he wouldn't have to work his ass off in a kitchen. Then he said that soon he would have lots of money. The next day, someone told me that some guy at Paradise Villas was robbed of a bunch of money he won at the

Grand Cayman Casino. Then I heard you and
Captain Hall talking in the hallway. You were
wondering how anyone could know the guy had so
much money. I asked Andrew if he had told anyone
about the guy on the boat and he got really nasty. He
said I should mind my own business."

Sanders mind was spinning. Could this be
the connection they had been looking for? He
needed to get Howie Hall over here to talk to
Tommy and Andrew right away.

"Okay, you may have a cause for concern,"
he finally said, trying to keep his voice steady. "So
what happened this morning?"

"This morning Andrew came in acting all
nervous and jumpy. He was really weirded out
about something. I asked if he was OK and he told
me to back off. Once breakfast was over, he came
up to me and apologized for being short with me.
Then he said he wanted to go see Skip and asked if I
would cover for him. He said he would be back in
an hour but he never showed up. Miss Marie and I
did all the lunch prep and lunch service. When we
finished, Miss Marie was really upset so I went to
look for him. There was no answer at Skip's room
so I came down and stopped at the desk. Like I told
you, Janie said he told her he was staying with Skip.
I went back to the kitchen hoping Andrew would be
there but he wasn't. That's when Miss Marie told
me you wanted to see me."

Tommy slumped in his seat like a deflated
balloon. Telling his story had taken a toll on him
physically and emotionally. He looked at Sanders,
worry and fear permeating his body.

"Mr. Sanders, do you think Andrew is involved?" Tommy asked.

"Honestly, I hope not, but we need to find him and have Captain Hall talk to both of you," Sanders replied. "You go back to the kitchen and help Miss Marie finish dinner prep. When you take your break afterward, stay close so I can find you."

Tommy stood and shook hands with Sanders. Although his face still looked worried, he seemed relieved now that he had told someone what he knew. He fled through the door as Sanders picked up the phone. He tried Julie's room again but there was no answer. He tried Skip's room with the same result. Finally, he called the police station and gave Captain Hall a brief version of his conversation with Tommy. Capt. Hall said he would be at the hotel shortly to talk to Tommy, Janie, and Andrew, if they could find him.

Sanders next stop was the front desk. Janie was still there talking to Michelle, the desk clerk on duty. She told Sanders the same story Tommy had told him about Andrew replacing her as Skip's "babysitter" for the morning. Apparently no one had seen Andrew since Janie left Skip's room. No one had seen Julie either. Michelle mentioned that Skip had never called down for lunch. When she called his room about one o'clock, there was no answer.

"Maybe Dr. Shelton was working with Skip on his physical therapy," Michelle guessed. "If they're in the middle of something, they might not take time to answer the phone. Normally they're done by noon so it was kind of weird. I figured Skip would call when he got hungry."

Hoping Michelle was right and physical therapy had taken longer than normal, Sanders took his pass-key and headed up to the third floor. He stopped first at Julie's room, knocked, and then let himself in when there was no answer. She was definitely not there but he noticed her backpack and bathing suit were sitting on the bed, ready for their afternoon activities. She never went anywhere without that backpack. It had gone with them every single afternoon.

He went down the hall to Skip's room. Again he knocked and had to let himself in when there was no answer. He entered the room to find Skip sound asleep in the bed. There was no sign of Julie and no sign that they had done any physical therapy. He studied the room for a minute and noticed a bottle of pain pills sitting on top of the room's mini-fridge. Now why would they be there instead of on the bedside table where they would be easy for Skip to reach? He was getting really worried and decided Skip was going to have to wake up to answer a few questions.

"Hey Skip," he said as he gently shook the boy's shoulder. "Time to wake up."

Skip mumbled something, pulled his arm away, and resettled himself in the bed. He shook Skip again, beginning to feel frantic for information.

"Skip," he said more forcefully. "Come on son, wake up. I need to talk to you."

Sanders shook Skip a little harder and Skip slowly opened his eyes. He blinked a couple of times and then started to drift off again. Sanders shook him again.

"Come on, wake up!" he shouted. "Wake up right now!"

"Okay, okay. Keep your pants on," Skip murmured as he rubbed his eyes.

After several more attempts, Sanders finally had Skip awake and sitting up. He gave Skip some water and brought him a wash cloth to scrub away the sleep. Skip was a little groggy but lucid.

"Sorry I told you to keep your pants on Mr. Sanders," he said sheepishly. "I was so tired I just couldn't get awake. I must have fallen asleep when Dr. Shelton was changing my bandages. All of the sudden I got so sleepy I couldn't keep my eyes open. I'm still tired....feel like I could sleep for hours. What time is it anyway?"

"It's two o'clock, Skip," Sanders answered. "When was Dr. Shelton here?"

"Are you kidding? Two o'clock in the afternoon?" Skip questioned. "That can't be right. No way I could have slept that long."

"Skip, I need you to focus for me," Sanders exclaimed. "What time was Dr. Shelton here? Was Andrew here with you then?"

"Uh, let's see. I had breakfast with Janie. She's really cute by the way. I might ask her out," Skip grinned then became serious. "Anyway, after breakfast, Andrew came up and told Janie she could leave. I don't think she wanted to go but he practically pushed her out the door. We were talking about my accident when Dr. Shelton showed up. Must have been about ten o'clock I guess. I don't remember for sure."

"Anything unusual happen before Dr. Shelton came by?" Sanders asked.

"Not that I can think of. I was talking to Andrew about the accident and how lucky I am that Dr. Shelton is staying here. I told him how awesome she is, how she comes by every morning to check on me and exercise my leg. I was really thirsty and asked him to get me a glass of juice. Janie was going to do it but I guess she forgot when Andrew showed up." Skip paused as he took a breath.

"After I asked a couple of times, Andrew finally fixed me some juice. I drank it and that's when Dr. Shelton came by. I was excited that I hadn't had any pain meds all night and she was happy for me. Let's see, I think that's when I got really sleepy. I remember they were talking about her accident while she was changing my bandages. Next thing I know, you were waking me up."

"Skip, why are your pain pills over there on top the fridge?" Sanders questioned.

"Got me," Skip responded. "They were here on the bedside table when I woke up this morning. I keep them close in case I need one at night. I don't want to be hopping around the room in the middle of the night looking for them."

Sanders began to pace across the room. Julie and Andrew had last been seen about ten o'clock and it was now two in the afternoon. Julie wouldn't go off somewhere by herself when they had made plans to explore Snipe Point. And where was Andrew? Something was very wrong. He could feel it in his gut. Telling Skip that he would send Janie up with lunch, he headed back to the front desk at a run.

Captain Hall arrived in the hotel lobby just as Sanders came flying through the stairwell door. His thoughts in turmoil, Sanders simply motioned for the policeman to follow him into his office. Once they were settled in seats, Sanders ran his hand over his face and let out a big sigh.

"Something's very wrong, Howie," he said in a rush, his voice revealing tremors of fear. "I can't find Julie anywhere. Skip was the last person to see her and Andrew. That was about ten o'clock this morning. Skip apparently fell asleep while she was changing his bandages and has been totally out of it for at least four hours. Andrew never came back to the kitchen for the lunch service. Too many things are out of whack!"

"Slow down Sanders," Captain Hall answered. "Let's start over so I get a full picture of the situation."

Sanders went slowly through what he knew, what Tommy and Skip had told him, and what he suspected. The more he spoke, the more worried he became. He stood up and began pacing the room. Again his gut told him something was very wrong.

"Alright, here's what we're going to do," Captain Hall said. "Send Tommy in and let me talk to him. While I'm doing that, get as much as your staff together as possible. I know you can't pull everyone in but do your best. We need to find out if anyone has seen Dr. Shelton or Andrew since this morning or if anyone saw anything unusual. Put them in the dining room since it's empty this time of day. I'll be in as soon as I finish with Tommy."

Sanders nodded and picked up the phone. He called Miss Marie and told her to send Tommy back again. Then he strode out of the room.

Twenty minutes later, about thirty staff members were assembled in the dining room. Front desk personnel, food servers, maid service, laundry staff, and maintenance men were all gathered together. The noise level in the room grew as they all talked at once wondering why they were there in the middle of the day. Full staff meetings were normally held early in the morning while the hotel's guests were still sleeping. Sanders and Captain Hall entered the room and the buzz quickly subsided.

"Thank you for gathering so quickly," Sanders began. "We have a small emergency and need your help. Captain Hall from the Little Cayman police is here and he has some information and some questions for you."

"Good afternoon everyone. We may have a guest and a staff member missing," Captain Hall said as he surveyed the room. "Dr. Shelton, the guest in Room 304, and Andrew from the kitchen staff were last seen about ten o'clock this morning in Skip's room. Skip fell asleep while they were there and doesn't know when they left. As far as we know, they haven't been seen since. Has anyone seen them or seen anything unusual today?"

The hotel staff members began to murmur to each other as they looked around the room. A lot of heads were shaking no and Sanders was beginning to think this had been a waste of time. Finally a hand shot up from the back of the room.

"Mr. Sanders, doesn't Andrew drive that old beat up car? You know, the one with crunched rear fenders and an engine that sounds like an airplane taking off?" a maintenance man asked.

The murmurs began again before anyone could answer, but this time heads were shaking yes. Tommy immediately shot to his feet from the chair he was sitting in at the back of the room.

"Yes he does, Jack!" he shouted over the heads of the crowd. "He normally parks it out back by the dumpster. I should go and see if it's there. Oh man I'm stupid. Why didn't I think of that before?"

"There's no need to go anywhere," Jack, the maintenance man replied. "I saw him peeling out of the lot this morning when I was taking the morning trash out to the dumpster. I just took the lunch trash out about ten minutes ago and that beat up piece of crap isn't there."

"Okay, I need you to stay behind when everyone leaves," Captain Hall said pointing to Jack. "Now did anyone else see anything? Has anyone seen Dr. Shelton today?"

Again the hotel staff began to murmur and shake their collective heads no. Sanders was growing more frantic by the moment. What could possibly have happened to Julie? Captain Hall asked a few more questions and when he was sure there was no more information to be gained from the remaining staff, he excused everyone except Tommy, Jack, and the rest of the maintenance staff. He told them to keep their eyes open for Dr. Shelton and Andrew and report in to Sanders if they saw either of them.

Once the crowd was cleared from the room, Captain Hall set the maintenance staff off to scour the entire hotel grounds for Dr. Shelton. They were instructed to search everywhere and ask any staff member not at the meeting if they had seen anything. He then sat down and talked to Jack about what he had seen earlier in the day. He confirmed through Tommy that the car Jack had seen was in fact Andrew's car. The only other information he gained was that it appeared there were three people in Andrew's car as it left the parking lot. The car was too far away and moving to fast for Jack to determine the identity of its occupants.

Captain Hall then excused Jack to join the search for Julie. Tommy was sent back to the kitchen and Miss Marie. The captain and Sanders decided to take a look at the parking lot and help with the grounds search. They strode out the back door and headed toward the dumpster. A quick survey of the area told them there wasn't much to see back there, so they turned to go back inside. As they did, Sanders caught a flash of light out of the corner of his eye.

"Hold on a second Howie," Sanders said as he moved toward the object that was catching the sun. His heart stopped when he saw what it was.

"Oh God no," he groaned as he picked up Julie's seahorse necklace from the pavement. "Howie, this is Julie's necklace. She wore it the first night we had dinner and several times after that too. There's no logical reason for it to be here unless they took her somewhere in Andrew's car. Howie, they have her!"

"Sanders, I hate to say so, but you just might be right," Captain Hall replied. "It's looking a lot like Andrew is mixed up with the robbers. I'm beginning to wonder if he somehow drugged Skip so they could take Dr. Shelton from the hotel."

"Skip said Andrew fixed him some juice and then he got really sleepy," Sanders noted. "His pain pills were sitting on top the fridge in his room when I went up earlier. He said he normally keeps them on the bedside table in easy reach. I would bet Andrew drugged Skip, but why would they take Julie?"

"I wish I had the answer to that. They must think she can identify them. Sanders, I think it's time I put out an APB on Andrew's car," the captain remarked. "We need to find that car and I'm betting we will find your lovely doctor nearby."

The men headed back to the hotel, Sanders more frightened than he had ever been in his life. The thought of Julie being in danger was like being kicked in the stomach over and over. He had to get her back. And then he had to tell her exactly how he felt about her.

CHAPTER 16

Julie was hungry, thirsty, and scared out of her mind. After forcing her into the car, Andrew and his friends had driven to the north side of the island. They went down a rutted road overgrown with weeds. At the end of the road was an abandoned shack. As she got out of the car, the tall one had hit her on the head from behind. She fell to her knees and tried to get back up. He hit her again and she blacked out.

When she came to, she realized she was tied to an old cast iron stove inside the shack. She could hear the three men standing outside discussing their escape from the island. From the sound of it, she would be going with them on a boat they were going to steal. They wanted to be out to sea before dark.

Closing her eyes for a few minutes, Julie tried to let her mind rest and think of a way out. Instead she suddenly understood the comment the short one had made about being a good swimmer. They were planning to throw her overboard once they got far enough away! In a panic, she started struggling with the ropes around her wrists. She was so frantic that she did not realize the men had come into the shack.

"Now just where do you think you're going pretty doctor?" the short squat one asked as he appeared in front of her. "I was in the Navy and know how to tie a knot. There's no way you're gonna get loose unless you're really, really nice to me! Want to know what would be really, really nice?"

"Leave her alone, Carl. She's not going anywhere," Andrew spoke as Julie went limp with fear. "We agreed nobody touches the doc until we're away from here. You can do whatever you want once we're on the water. Then we can dump her over the side, never to be found again."

"Yeah, yeah I know," Carl muttered. "But a guy can dream can't he?"

"That's about all you can do, you dumb hick," the tall man laughed. "You wouldn't know what to do with a beautiful woman if she fell into your lap!"

"Shut up, Darren!" Carl shouted as he lunged at the tall man.

The two men scuffled for a few minutes until Andrew finally pulled them apart. They were both still hurling muffled insults as they walked to opposite sides of the shack. Andrew looked at Julie for a moment, then turned and walked away. He looked scared out of his wits.

"Our time is really limited you idiots!" Andrew shouted. "Once they figure out the doc here is gone, Mr. Sanders is gonna pull out all the stops to find her. You two need to steal the boat right now. I'll stay here. My face is too well known around the island. Come back here when the boat is tied up at that abandoned dock and help me. I sure don't want to loose either the money or the doc somewhere in the woods."

Darren turned to Andrew with the most menacing look Julie had ever seen.

"When did you become the leader of our little team?" he sneered. "I'm the idea man here, so don't tell me what to do!"

"I'm not telling you what to do," Andrew replied, his voice trembling. "I just want to get off this miserable island and that's never gonna happen if you and Carl are arguing over Dr. Shelton. She's our ticket out of here, but only if she's alive and well."

"As long as you know who the boss is, Andy boy." Darren gave Andrew another menacing look.

Darren and Carl headed out the door mumbling insults at each other. Andrew sat on an old milk crate and started biting his nails. Julie thought he looked almost as frightened as she felt. Maybe she could talk some sense into him while the other two were gone.

"Andrew, can we talk about this?" Julie began. "I don't know how you got mixed up with these guys, but don't let them drag you down any farther."

"Just be quiet Dr. Shelton," Andrew grumbled.

"Right now the most the police can hold you for is being an accessory to robbery. And who knows, maybe they will drop the charges if you testify against the other guys," she continued. "Don't let them get you involved in murder. A little bit of money isn't worth it, Andrew."

"*SHUT UP,* Dr. Shelton!" Andrew yelled as he began pacing around the room. "You don't know anything about it. Just shut up!!"

"Tell me about it, Andrew" Julie said softly. "I'm a doctor. I listen to my patient's problems all the time."

"Well, it's like this pretty lady," Andrew replied. "If I let you go or mess up in any way at all, Darren will slice me up. If I turn them in, Darren will tell the police I was the ring leader and ran the show. Then once I end up in prison, he will find a way to kill me. He's done time for using his knife to carve up a gangbanger who refused to give up his money. You don't know him. He's ruthless, totally ruthless. I have no choice. It's your life or mine. So just shut up!"

Andrew stormed out of the shack, leaving Julie alone with her thoughts. She had to figure out a way to get loose. She tried to think things through, but her thoughts were all jumbled. Her head hurt like fire and her stomach was queasy. She began to wonder if she had a concussion from being hit on the head. Taking deep breaths, she closed her eyes and tried to relax.

Julie suddenly heard voices outside the shack and realized she had fallen asleep. She had no idea how long she had been out. Not a good thing if I have a head injury she thought. She heard them talking about how easy it was to steal the boat. They were excited that they found another $2000 stashed in a lock box on the boat. Finally, Andrew came back inside followed by the other two men. They were in a big rush now as they gathered duffel bags and prepared to leave.

When they were ready, Darren came over to the stove and cut the ropes from Julie's wrists. She

CAYMAN KISS

stood and was assailed by a giant wave of dizziness.
She grabbed the edge of the stove for support and
held her stomach as nausea swept through her body.
The tall man jerked her by the arm and pushed her
into the center of the shack.

"All right doc. Let's go. No pretending to be
sick. We don't have time," Darren growled.

"I'm not pretending. You hit me pretty hard
and I may have a concussion," Julie replied as anger
engulfed her. "Give me a minute to get my head
together."

"Andrew, tie her hands behind her back and
let's get going," Darren ordered. "We have about
two hours of daylight left. I want to be well out to
sea by dark."

They hustled Julie out the door and into the
car. Once again she was forced to sit on the floor so
her head would be below window level. After a
short drive, the car stopped and the men got out.
Carl had been in the back seat and pulled her roughly
out the door. He took a moment to put his hand on
her breast. He looked at her with dead eyes and she
shuddered with fear.

"Come on you idiot," Darren yelled. "You
can feel up the doc when we get out on the ocean.
Right now we have to get on the boat and head out to
sea."

Carl grumbled under his breath and pushed
Julie forward toward a boat tied up at the abandoned
dock. It was the only boat there. There was nothing
else in sight and Julie felt panic engulf her body.
How could she die without telling Sanders that she
loved him? Why would her time on this earth end

now when she had just discovered what real love was? She knew deep inside that Sanders would be looking for her, but she couldn't just sit and wait. She had to try to get away before they got on the boat.

Another hard push on her back brought Julie back to reality. She stumbled forward toward the dock, her mind working to find a way out. She looked around at her surroundings but there was nothing except the dock. This part of the island was sparsely inhabited and the dock was hidden from view by a stand of beautiful mahogany trees. Swallowing her rising panic, Julie decided her only chance was to get to the road and run until a car came by. She dragged her feet, letting Andrew and Darren get further ahead. When Carl stepped slightly in front of her to ask Darren a question, she took the opportunity to turn and run.

Running as fast as her splitting head would allow, Julie headed out the gravel road toward the main road. She was glad she had some endurance from jogging as she ran for her life. The men suddenly realized she was making a break for it and they began shouting at each other. Hoping to gain a lead while they argued, she sprinted faster toward the main road. Just as she reached the intersection, a hand grabbed her arm and spun her around.

"You stupid bitch!" Darren screamed at her as he backhanded her across the face. "You're not going anywhere!!"

Julie fell in the gravel, scraping her legs and arms and reeling with dizziness. Darren grabbed her arm and jerked her to her feet. Cursing a blue streak, he dragged her all the way to the dock. Without a word, he picked her up and threw her onto the boat. Julie landed hard on her back, breath rushing out of her. The three men climbed onto the boat and prepared to head out to the open ocean. They left Julie lying on the bottom of the boat, dizzy and barely conscious. Within minutes, the boat was bouncing over the waves in the inlet, its nose pointing toward the open ocean.

Back at the Sunset Inn, the scene was organized chaos. Little Cayman police, locals who had adopted Sanders as family, and hotel staff were being briefed on what was known about Andrew's car in preparation for an island wide search. They were split up in groups of four and assigned an area of the island to search. Sanders was filled with terror but warmed by the turnout of locals who wanted to help. Even Granny Lele was there, helping Miss Marie hand out cups of coffee and words of wisdom.

"Mr. Sanders!" Haley, the afternoon desk clerk, shouted over the din of voices in the lobby. "Suzette from the police station needs to talk to Captain Hall immediately. She's really upset about something!"

The police captain strode to the desk and took the phone. He spoke briefly to Suzette and then hurried back to Sanders.

"Jimmy Capstone at Little C Divers just reported that his boat was stolen. He's a small operation on the north side of the island. Only has the one boat. He off-loaded his last dive group and went home for a bite to eat. He went back to do some clean up and the boat was gone along with today's receipts. He only accepts cash so they got about $2000."

"Well at least now we know how they plan to get off the island," Sanders said. "We have to find that boat Howie. What if they dump Julie into the ocean? She'll never make it!"

"I know, Sanders, I know," Captain Hall replied. "I'm sending my guys to check every dock on the island whether used or abandoned. They will start at Little C and go in both directions from there. There isn't much else I can do."

"But there is something I can do," Sanders offered. "I'm calling my buddy with the helicopter. He can be here in twenty minutes and cover the entire island in another twenty."

"You do that while I get my men started," he answered and went off to the group of police officers standing to the side.

By the time Sanders had arranged for the helicopter, the small police force was on it's way to the north side of the island to search every dock on Little Cayman. Sanders went out to the beach, pacing up and down while he waited for the helicopter to arrive. He had to find Julie and get her back alive. No other outcome was an option in his mind. He had to tell her that he loved her and then he had to ask her to marry him and live on Little Cayman. He felt like time was standing still until he heard the roar of the helicopter as it approached the beach. He watched as the copter touched down and then headed towards it at a run.

"Steve, thank you so much for this," Sanders exclaimed as he climbed in beside the pilot.

"No problem, Sanders," the pilot replied. "Anything new since we spoke?"

"Nothing," Sanders said. "Let's head toward the north side of the island, tracking along the beach. Howie Hall and his men are checking out docks over there since that's where the boat was stolen."

The giant bird revved up her engines and lifted into the sky. It skimmed along the water near the beach as it headed around the western tip of the island. Sanders was scanning the coast line and as far inland as possible with a pair of binoculars he had brought along. They had just started up the northern coast when the radio crackled to life.

"Sanders, it's Howie," a voice said in the headphones Sanders was wearing. "We just found Andrew's car at an abandoned dock on the northeast corner of the island. Nobody in it and nobody anywhere around. They must have taken off already."

"We're headed that way now," Sanders replied, his gut clenching in dread. "They must have Julie with them. Can you get a boat up there while we look around?"

"Already on the way," Captain Hall answered. "You guys find them and my men and I will take them down."

"Just remember that Julie is probably on that boat," Sanders cried, his voice cracking with emotion. "Don't let anything happen to her."

"I know Sanders," the police captain responded. "We'll do everything we can to keep her safe. I need you and that whirlybird to stay in the area in case we need help."

"Don't worry, I'm not going anywhere until she's out of danger. If they've hurt her at all, you may have to put me in jail for assault or, more likely, murder."

Captain Hall was surprised at the thought that his friend had finally found someone who could heal his heart. After the mess in Texas, he didn't think Sanders would ever fall in love again. Dr. Shelton must be a very special woman to get under Sanders' skin like she had. They absolutely needed to save this incredible lady or Sanders would never survive.

"Keep this channel open Sanders," he said. "If you see the boat, give me the coordinates so we can shut them down. We only have a little over an hour of daylight left. Tracking them after dark will be nearly impossible."

"Got it," Sanders noted as he resumed scanning with the binoculars.

The helicopter scooted up the north coast of Little Cayman as Sanders' head swiveled back and forth, searching for the woman he loved. His stomach was rolling as he thought of Julie in the hands of such vicious men. His worst fear was that they would dump her in the ocean and he would never see her again. They soon passed the dock where Little C Divers berthed its boat. Minutes later, he saw a police boat pulling up to a dock where an old beat up car was surrounded by police cars. Sanders nearly buckled over at the sight but quickly steeled himself to finish the search.

Julie was still lying in the bottom of the boat, nauseous and dizzy. The boat was racing along at top speed as the men tried to get as far away from

Little Cayman as possible. They had about an hour of daylight left and then would have to cut back on the speed to navigate the ocean waters in the dark. She had heard them talking and discovered they had almost $20,000 from robberies on Little Cayman and Grand Cayman. She also learned that Carl had plans for her once darkness set in.....plans she wouldn't enjoy. Suddenly, drowning in the ocean sounded much more appealing than staying aboard the dive boat.

Struggling because her hands were still tied, Julie finally sat up in the bouncing boat. The men were huddled at the controls, pushing the engine as hard as possible. She surveyed the boat looking for something to cut the rope with. If she could get the bindings off, she might have a small chance of surviving when she jumped into the ocean. She had decided that under no circumstances would she remain in this boat after dark. She found a rough edge on one of the metal storage boxes and backed up to it. She began to quietly saw the ropes circling her wrists against the sharp metal.

Just as the rope snapped, Carl turned around and gave Julie a menacing grin. He walked to the back of the boat and stood in front of her. He reached out and ran a hand across her hair causing Julie to shrink back in fear and disgust. Enraged by her reaction, he squatted down and got in her face. His eyes were wild with hatred and violence.

"Look Dr. Bitch," Carl muttered. "You better show me some respect or you're gonna hurt real bad before you go swimming with the sharks. Be nice to me, enjoy what we're gonna do, and you can go to your death with a smile on your face."

Julie felt bile rise in her throat. Everything about this man revolted her. She resolved once again to jump off the boat before it got dark. She closed her eyes and prayed for Sanders to find her before it was too late. Carl stood up and moved away.

Breathing a sigh of relief, Julie began to plan her escape to the deep ocean waters. With her wrists free, she might be able to grab a life jacket and stay afloat. Trying not to think about sharks, she scanned the boat again, this time looking for a suitable flotation device. Her eyes landed on a pile of gear on the other side of the boat. She saw several life vests mixed in with wet suits. Thank goodness the boat captain hadn't completed his clean up today!

Suddenly the sky was filled with a droning sound. Julie looked around to see a big helicopter coming toward them. The giant copter circled at a distance and she could see someone leaning out, spying on them with binoculars. Andrew, Carl, and Darren were frantically working the controls, pushing the boat harder as they tried to get away from the helicopter. Realizing this was her chance, Julie stood and fought a wave of nausea. Crossing to the other side of the boat, she stole a quick glance at her kidnappers. Fearing they would see her frenzied movements, she quickly grabbed two life vests off the pile she had spied. With a final look over her shoulder, Julie leaped into the cold sea water.

Up in the helicopter, Sanders was looking at the boat, trying to determine if it was the missing Little C dive boat. He was urging the pilot to get closer when his binoculars caught sight of a woman. He screamed Julie's name as she crossed the boat, grabbed something, and jumped over the side. Knowing how scared she was to have water over her head, Sanders was struck by a fear so profound he almost blacked out. She had chosen the ocean over whatever was happening in that boat. That could only mean she was so terrified of the men in the boat, her fear of water took a back seat.

"Steve, get over there now!" Sanders shouted. "Julie just jumped overboard. I have to get to her before she panics and drowns!!"

"On the way, my friend," Steve responded as he banked the chopper and headed directly at the boat.

The helicopter closed in on the boat, whipping up waves. Julie held tight to the two life jackets she had grabbed as she went overboard. She saw Sanders barking instructions to the helicopter pilot and then watched as the copter dropped lower. When it was ten feet above the water, Sanders jumped and disappeared into the ocean. As soon as he was in the water, a bulky bag dropped from the helicopter, landing in the water behind him. He surfaced, found the floating bag, and began swimming toward her. The helicopter lifted upward and began tracking after the racing boat.

It took Sanders just two minutes to reach Julie….the longest two minutes of his life. He put his arms around her and held her against his chest as

173

they treaded water. He finally let go and pulled a cord on the side of the bag. The "bag" inflated and Julie realized it was a life raft. She never thought she would be so happy to see a tiny raft in the middle of the ocean. Sanders helped her into the raft and climbed in beside her. They clung to each other as they watched two police boats race past, heading towards the stolen dive boat. The only words spoken came from Sanders.

"Oh God, I thought I lost you," he murmured as he held her tight. "I can't lose you my love. Not now, not ever."

CHAPTER 17

Julie opened her eyes to sunlight streaming in through the sliding glass doors of her hotel room. For a few minutes she lay quietly, thinking that while her vacation was almost over, she had enjoyed it immensely. Then the events of yesterday came crashing back to her and she choked on the tears that began streaming from her eyes. Hearing her sobs, Sanders jumped up from the sofa and rushed to the bed. He pulled her to his chest and held her tenderly until the wave of tears subsided.

"I'm sorry," she whispered. "I'm such a baby."

"You were kidnapped, tied up, threatened with rape and murder, and almost drowned," Sanders said in a soft voice. "I think you're entitled to some tears, Darlin'."

At that moment, Julie remembered what Sanders had said in the life raft as they waited for a police boat to pick them up. Her heart filled with such love she thought it might explode and the tears began again. He had said he didn't want to ever lose her. She had felt his love for her as they held each other. Every fiber of his being had reached out to her and she knew they were meant to be together. As if he heard her thoughts, Sanders pulled back and looked deep into her eyes. The love she saw in them must certainly mirror her own.

"How are you feeling?" Sanders asked without taking his eyes from hers. "You were pretty restless all night and all morning. I didn't have to worry about waking you up to check for a concussion. You woke up every few hours on your own."

"I'm okay I think," Julie responded. "I was having nightmares about that creepy Carl and what he kept threatening to do to me. I'm still shocked that I chose to jump into the ocean over staying on that boat another minute. I thought if I was going to be shark bait anyway, there was no reason to wait until after I had been raped."

"When I saw you go over the side of the boat on your own, I knew you must be frightened out of your mind," Sanders said. "And I also knew that I had to do whatever it took to get you out of that water. Julie, the thought of you drowning and being gone forever from my life was like being stabbed in my heart. I love you more than life itself. I never thought I could feel this way for anyone, especially someone I've known for such a short time. But I love you deeply and I need you to know that my heart belongs to you now and always."

"Sanders, I never imagined my vacation would turn out like this, but I wouldn't change a thing," Julie said with tears in her eyes. "I found the man of my dreams in an exquisitely beautiful place. A place that I didn't even know existed until a month ago. I love you with all my heart and always will."

"So what are we going to do about it?" he asked. "I'm not much for long distance relationships."

"What do you want to do about it?" Julie asked looking directly into Sanders eyes.

"Honestly? I want you to live here with me. I want you to be the medical director of the new clinic. I want to spend every night holding you in my arms and making wild, passionate love with you. And I hope with all my heart that you want that too."

"I've never wanted anything as much as I want to be with you," she answered, a huge smile creasing her face. "Being with the man I love, living on an beautiful island, and having my own medical clinic is more than I ever dreamed of. I'll have to go to Chicago and wrap things up but I'll be back. You can count on it."

Sanders took Julie's face in his hands and kissed her so gently it felt like a butterfly caressing her lips. The kiss was the softest, sweetest, sexiest kiss she had ever experienced. Despite her aching head and scraped arms and legs, she felt fabulous. When he finally pulled away, they both sighed.

"I hate to leave you, but I have some things to do to keep this hotel running," he said. "Why don't you get up and see if you're still dizzy or nauseous?"

Julie slowly stood and was surprised when she felt steady on her feet. She took a few steps to be sure. Aside from a small residual headache, everything seemed to be in working order. Her stomach agreed as it growled to be fed. Her ordeal yesterday had left her so exhausted that all she had wanted to do last night was sleep the horror of the day away. Sanders laughed as her stomach made its needs known a second time.

"I think when I go downstairs I'd better have Miss Marie send you some lunch," he chuckled.

"That stomach of yours is certainly making a racket!"

"Well the last meal I had was breakfast with you yesterday morning," she replied with a chuckle of her own. "Since I took a detour out to sea and then slept for fifteen hours straight when I got back, I missed three of Miss Marie's delicious meals. Give me time to take a shower and get dressed first before you send food up. Maybe fifteen minutes."

"No problem, Darlin'," Sanders responded, his face soft with love. "Once you eat, stick close to the hotel please. I want to keep an eye on you until I'm sure you're okay."

"I'm going to make a few phone calls to Chicago and then spend some time on the beach. Oh, I should probably check on Skip too," she replied. "I've neglected my first Little Cayman patient!"

"I snuck out awhile ago and checked on him. He's doing fine. He is very happy you weren't hurt and the robbers have been caught. Now before I leave, do you need anything else?"

"I do need one thing," Julie said.

She walked over to Sanders and put her arms around him. He pulled her against his body as she nestled against his chest. Once again they both sighed in contentment. Julie raised her head and looked up at him. He placed his lips on hers and kissed her with such passion she felt like she was floating off the floor. This kiss was a mirror of the one he had given her just moments before, a kiss that filled her heart and soul with love and heated her entire body. After several long minutes, Sanders finally broke the kiss.

"Darlin'," he whispered. "I can't wait until you're here for good and I can kiss your lips a few dozen times a day."

"Me too," she whispered back to him. "Me too….."

Sanders left Julie to her shower and headed out the door. She cleaned up and had a delicious lunch delivered personally by Miss Marie. Miss Marie stayed while Julie ate, thanking her over and over for risking her life to help Tommy. When she finished her meal, the two ladies left the room together. At the elevator, Miss Marie looked knowingly at Julie.

"Granny Lele said to tell you that she is very happy we're going to have a woman doctor on the island. And I'm happy Mr. Sanders will have someone special in his life. He's a good man and deserves a good woman like you," Miss Marie said with a twinkle in her eye.

"How did you……oh forget it. You and Granny Lele know more than anyone else on this island," Julie replied. "I don't know how you know so much, but you do, so let me just say thank you. Sanders is the man of my dreams and I'm the luckiest woman in the world. Tell Granny Lele that it will be my pleasure to treat her and everyone else on this fabulous island that I'll be calling home very soon."

Miss Marie beamed a huge smile and nodded as they entered the elevator. She kept eyeing Julie as they rode together to the hotel lobby. When they stepped out, Miss Marie stopped and put a hand on her arm.

"I hope you decide to hold the wedding here. It would bring me great pleasure to prepare a magnificent wedding feast for you, she said.

"I think you're getting a little ahead of things," Julie replied. "We talked about me moving here, but Sanders hasn't asked me to marry him."

"Oh he will," Miss Marie responded as she enveloped Julie in a warm hug.

Julie stepped back and smiled. She started to say something, but decided it was fruitless. Miss Marie and Granny Lele were certainly in the know about so many things that all she could do is hope they were right. She wanted to marry Sanders and begin a new life here in this paradise.

She walked across the lobby towards the beach. Every few feet she was stopped by hotel staff members. They all inquired about how she was feeling and thanked her for helping to catch the robbers. After a fifteen minute trip across the small lobby, Julie finally headed to the beach. It took her almost as long to go down the path, pass the tiki bar, and find a chair on the beach as it did to get through the hotel lobby. Again, hotel staffers were quite interested in her health and very glad the traitor amongst them had been caught. Julie was struck by how these people took care of each other like they were all family. She couldn't wait to begin her new life here!

As she settled on her beach chair, Julie's heart was soaring. She closed her eyes while she thought about Sanders. The heat from the sun felt so good on her battered body that she was soon drowsing under the umbrella. She had no idea how long she had been sleeping when she sensed a cooling of the air. She wondered why the sun was suddenly dimmed.

Julie cracked one eye open to see if it had gotten cloudy. An extremely well built, light haired man was standing at the foot of the chair, peering down at her. The sun was setting and Julie couldn't see his face, but she felt his piercing stare as he looked up and down her body. Julie sat up straighter and shielded her eyes with one hand to get a better look. Sanders was standing there looking at her with eyes full of love. He took her hand and pulled her to her feet. He slowly brushed his lips against hers. Julie felt her entire body shiver. It was a simple kiss but it was the most sensual feeling in the world.

"Come," he commanded in a soft but firm voice.

Julie nodded her head once and, holding his hand like it was a lifeline, walked back toward the hotel. The lush foliage surrounding the little hotel went unnoticed as they walked up the sandy path and down the tiled walkway past the pool. The chatter and laughter of the pool patrons was nothing but background noise now. The only thing Julie could focus on was the extreme heat radiating from his hand into her hand and rapidly diffusing through her entire body. Her skin was flushed, her nipples were hard, and she could feel a heaviness building in her lower stomach.

They reached the lobby and turned toward Sanders' apartment. Outside the door, Sanders once again brushed his lips over hers. Julie's entire body tingled from the soft kiss. She had never before been so turned on from a kiss. He opened the apartment door and let Julie enter first.

"Oh God," she thought. "I want him to kiss me and touch me until I scream. I need him inside me, right now."

As if he heard her thoughts, he closed the door, pulled her to him, and gently placed his lips against hers. An electric current shot through her body and she felt wetness forming between her legs. His tongue gently pried her lips open and thrust into her mouth. The sensation of his tongue touching hers made Julie's legs go weak. Just when she thought her legs would give way completely, he stepped back and took her hand once again. As they crossed the room, Julie realized Sanders was the light haired man in the dream she had just before deciding to make this trip. Yes, he was most definitely the man of her dreams she thought with a smile.

They crossed the living room and Sanders said dinner would be arriving shortly. He asked if she wanted wine but she replied that first she wanted a shower and change of clothes.

"I knew you would want a shower before dinner," he laughed. "I hope you don't mind that I let myself into your room. A selection of clothes is waiting for you in the bathroom along with some toiletries. Take your time. I'll be here when you're done."

Julie took a long, luxurious shower, feeling her muscles relax in the hot water. She toweled her hair dry and dressed. When she opened the door, Sanders was standing at the kitchen island waiting for her. He smiled, took her hand, and led her out the sliding door to his terrace. She saw a table set for dinner for two complete with wine, lighted candles, and flowers. Sanders took her in his arms once more and kissed her deeply. He broke the kiss and guided her to the table. He held the chair for her as she sat and then he sat down too. Julie sensed a slight nervousness in his manner and she wondered if he might be having second thoughts about his offer from this morning.

"How are you feeling?" Sanders asked, his voice carrying an anxious edge. "Any dizziness or nausea today?"

"No, I'm feeling wonderful," Julie answered, her eyes full of love for this man. "Some minor aches but considering I was tied up, dragged across a parking lot, and jumped into the ocean, I'm doing quite well."

"Good, good," he replied sounding even more nervous now.

"Sanders, are you okay?" she inquired.

"Of course," he said. "Of course. I just need to say something to you and I'm not sure how to begin."

He suddenly jumped up from his chair and came around to hers. She looked up into his eyes and love once again poured from them. So what was he so apprehensive about? He offered his hand so she stood and looked directly at him. He smiled and dropped to one knee. He pulled a jewelry box from his pocket.

"Julie Shelton, will you marry me? I love you with all my being and the only thing that could possibly make me happier is if you would be my wife. Please say you will marry me."

"Yes, Simon Sanders, I'll marry you," Julie responded. "I would be thrilled and honored to be your wife."

Sanders opened the jewelry box and withdrew an incredibly beautiful diamond ring. He placed it on her finger and then turned her hand and slowly kissed her palm. Julie drew in a deep breath as heat once again shot through her body.

"It's absolutely beautiful," she whispered. "Where did you get such an amazing piece of jewelry on this tiny island?"

"This ring belonged to my grandmother," Sanders said. "She left it to me when she died and I've been keeping it for the right woman. You're the right woman to wear something this elegant and beautiful, Julie. You're the only woman for me, Darlin'."

"Oh Sanders," Julie cried. "I love you so much!"

Sanders stood and she wrapped her arms around his neck and buried her head in his chest. He smiled hugely and held her tight. When she pulled back to look up at him, he leaned down and softly kissed her lush, ripe lips. The resulting electric current rushed through both of them and the kiss became even more passionate. Julie was suddenly frantic to feel his skin against hers, feel his lips move over her body. She broke the embrace and took his hand.

"I know Miss Marie made a special dinner for me but I'm suddenly not very hungry," she whispered. "The only thing I'm hungry for right now is you."

They made their way to the bedroom and Sanders stopped Julie at the bedside. He kissed her again, so softly she barely felt the contact on her lips but her body felt it and she turned to molten heat inside. His hands slid slowly down both arms and back up again making her shiver.

"I want to see your magnificent body," he whispered as he broke the kiss.

Sanders' fingers slid the spaghetti straps of her dress down and he kissed her neck, her shoulders, and then the tops of her breasts. Julie's breathing became ragged as her breasts swelled and her nipples hardened. He reached behind her and slid the zipper down with one hand while the fingers of his other hand trailed down her spine. She gasped when his fingers gently caressed the small of her back and brushed the top of her thong panties.

With a single motion, Sanders swept her dress to the floor and placed his hands on her naked breasts. He heard her sharp intake of breath as he gently squeezed her swollen breasts and ran his fingertips over her hard nipples. She moaned softly and he felt her entire body shiver in pleasure. Julie's response to his slightest touch was so erotic that it took his breath away.

He moved his hands slowly down her sides until his fingertips reached her thong. He knelt before her and kissed the spot on her belly just above the thong. His tongue slid across her skin, up to her belly button, and back down to the top of her thong. He knew she was wet, he could smell her arousal. He lost himself in her scent for a few moments, wanting this to last forever.

A moan escaped Julie's lips bringing Sanders back to the moment. He realized he had been licking her belly just where the thong touched her skin. He took his time as he slid the tiny scrap of fabric over her hips and dropped it to the floor. His hands went around her, gently grabbing her butt, as he pressed his face into her soft pubic hair. He inhaled her scent and knew what heaven was like.

He slid his hands over her butt and down her the back of her thighs. She instinctively spread her legs, needing him, needing the release only he could provide. Sanders' tongue darted out, flicking against her hard clit once, twice, again and again and again. Julie moaned louder and put her hands on his shoulders to steady herself. He grabbed her butt cheeks again and pressed her into his hot, wet, needy tongue. She screamed his name and the first orgasm burst out of her, followed quickly by the second and third.

When the waves of pleasure subsided, Sanders rose and kissed her hard. Julie tasted herself on his tongue and lips. It was like taking an aphrodisiac. She needed to taste him, smell his skin, feel his penis throbbing inside her. She slowly, seductively unbuttoned the white dress shirt he was wearing. Her lips pressed against his powerful chest as her hands slide up his torso to his shoulders. She licked and kissed her way up to his neck and then slid his shirt off his massive shoulders. It joined her dress and panties on the floor.

Julie's hands glided back down over his chest and stomach until they found the button on his pants. She unbuttoned his pants, slid the zipper down, and pushed his pants to the floor. His hard penis sprang free and she wrapped one hand around it. She began stroking him with one hand, pressing her naked belly against the other side of his throbbing shaft. He groaned as her hand moved up and down on one side of his penis while the other side was burrowing against the soft, white hot skin of her stomach. He lowered his head and kissed her as if his life depended on it.

When she removed her lips from his he shook his head and moaned a long noooooo. Julie barely heard him. She had to taste him, take his hard length into her mouth. She knelt in front of him and licked his hardness from his balls up to the head. Her hands cupped his swollen balls as she took him into her steaming hot mouth. She sucked him into her mouth and down her throat. He groaned again and then relaxed into the sensual rhythm of being sucked deep into her throat and sliding slowly back out as her hands massaged his balls. He was close, so close to orgasm that he was almost lost. But he couldn't come yet, not until he was buried deep inside her, her heat and wetness enveloping every inch of him.

"Oh God baby, that is too good," Sanders whispered. "I need to be inside you Julie. Now, right now."

He reached down as her mouth released him and pulled her to her feet. He lifted her in his arms, stealing a quick kiss, and then licking a hard nipple as he gently laid her on the bed. He stood at the side of the bed and looked at her perfect body. Her chest rose and fell as her breath came in short bursts. Her swollen breasts beckoned him as they moved with the rhythm of her breathing. He looked into her eyes and saw love, desire, and total commitment to him. His return look was a mirror of hers.

Sanders climbed onto the bed and positioned himself at Julie's feet. He licked her toes, her ankles, and slid his tongue up the inside of her legs. When he reached the dark, heated V between her legs, she was quivering and moaning in pure bliss. He spread her legs farther apart and his tongue once again touched her clit. She grabbed the sheets as she arched up, shuddering with a giant, all-consuming orgasm. He continued to lick her clit and pussy lips until she was writhing with nonstop orgasms. He plunged his tongue into her, tasting her erotic wetness and making her come again and again.

Finally he began to move upward, his wet tongue gliding up her belly and over her breasts. He licked her nipples and suckled each swollen breast until she was panting again with need. He was rock hard and pressed against her leg, in awe of the way she responded to his touch, his tongue. She was his dream woman.....sensual, unafraid of her sexuality, making her needs as well as her pleasure known. He could wait no longer. He had to be inside her.

Sanders moved up and lay on top of Julie, wanting to be inside her, feel her heat, make her scream his name again. He kissed her, running his tongue over her lips and then sliding it into her mouth. She moved beneath him, spreading her legs, making her own need known. He raised his head and looked into her eyes. His eyes were black with desire and love.

"I love you," he whispered.

"I love you too," she whispered in return.

His eyes locked onto hers as he entered her heated core. She moaned softly and he nearly lost control. He took a deep breath and began to move slowly inside her, stroking her with his throbbing rock hard shaft. His entire body was on fire. His skin burned where it was pressed against her from chest to pelvis. His hands slid up her arms and clasped her hands, the skin burning where they touched. He moved inside her a little faster, unable to help himself.

Julie was lost in the incredible sensation of Sanders' hot, hard penis moving inside her. She couldn't think, couldn't speak. All she could do was feel as he pushed up into her, her body contracting around him, trying to keep him inside her forever. As the pace of his thrusts increased, her pleasure increased even more until she was coming over and over again. Her legs spread even wider, wanting to take all of him into her heat and wetness.

He continued to thrust into her until finally he groaned and shouted her name. He came, buried deep inside her, his brain able to focus only on the incredible intensity of his orgasm. The sound of her name escaping Sanders' lips pushed Julie even higher. Sensing the depth of his orgasm sent her over the edge once again. She came, screaming his name and pulling him tighter against her body and deeper into her pussy.

They lay completely entwined, neither wanting to break the spell of the most erotic, sensual experience of their lives. Minutes passed as they slowly came back to reality. Sanders finally raised his head and looked once again into her eyes.

"I never knew it could be like this," he said softly. "I love you Julie and promise to do whatever it takes to make you happy. I want you with me always."

"You make me happy Sanders and I love you with every breath I take, every beat of my heart," Julie replied. "You have me now and forever."

Miss Marie's dinner forgotten, they held each other as they fell into a deep, deep sleep.

THE END

*Did you enjoy **Cayman Kiss**? I would love to hear your comments about my first contemporary romance novel. Please go to Amazon.com and write a brief review.*

Thank you!

Jaqueline Kiss

Find me on the web at:

JaquelineKissBooks.com

Watch for **Carolina Kiss**,

a new Jaqueline Kiss book due out soon!

www.ingramcontent.com/pod-product-compliance
Lightning Source LLC
Chambersburg PA
CBHW071233130626
46556CB00003B/993